"YOU'RE GOING TO BE SEEING A LOT OF ME."

"Really?" Vickie replied. "Your confidence is amazing."

Brant shrugged. "Maybe. But I wouldn't suggest a wager against me. I want you, my sweet leading lady, and I intend to get you."

"I thought you hadn't asked me to bed?"

"I haven't—yet. We're going to start with basics."

"You'll excuse me if I don't happen to be around for your basics, since I've made it clear I'm not interested in the finale."

Brant's annoying, knowing grin never left his face. His blue eyes raked over her form in a probing, assessing gaze.

"You'll be around. We both know it. The only one you're lying to is yourself. Why, I don't know. But I think I've already solved half of my dilemma. You're afraid of me. Now the question is why?"

A CANDLELIGHT ECSTASY ROMANCE ®

TENDER DECEPTION

Heather Graham

A CANDLELIGHT ECSTASY ROMANCE ®

Published by
Dell Publishing Co., Inc.
1 Dag Hammarskjold Plaza
New York, New York 10017

For Gwen and Barney

Dell ® TM 681510, Dell Publishing Co., Inc.

Candlelight Ecstasy Romance®, 1,203,540, is a registered
trademark of Dell Publishing Co., Inc.,
New York, New York.

ISBN: 0–440–18591–2

Printed in the United States of America
First printing—February 1984

To Our Readers:

We have been delighted with your enthusiastic response to Candlelight Ecstasy Romances®, and we thank you for the interest you have shown in this exciting series.

In the upcoming months we will continue to present the distinctive sensuous love stories you have come to expect only from Ecstasy. We look forward to bringing you many more books from your favorite authors and also the very finest work from new authors of contemporary romantic fiction.

As always, we are striving to present the unique, absorbing love stories that you enjoy most—books that are more than ordinary romance.

Your suggestions and comments are always welcome. Please write to us at the address below.

Sincerely,

The Editors
Candlelight Romances
1 Dag Hammarskjold Plaza
New York, New York 10017

PROLOGUE

She was young in years and in experience when she stood at his doorstep that night. She was at that age when the tender blossom of youth had flowered delicately into womanhood; her skin was soft and smooth, radiating the purity of alabaster, her body lithesome, tall, perfect, willowy, slim, curvaceous, innocently provocative.

She hadn't come to seduce; indeed, such an idea would have never entered her head. Yet she had come as a temptress, innately drawing upon her feminine wiles. Dressed in a stunning, sultry silk sheath, her blue-black hair cropped in a sophisticated swing, she appeared far older than her years. She moved with an effort-less grace, a grace finely honed to perfection from the training that she had embraced in her search for her dream.

He was another dream, not a fixed vision, but a vague dream. She didn't see a pretty white house with a picket fence, nor imagine a rose-tinted wedding when she thought of him.

She had come because she loved him with a naive simplicity. He was upset; he was alone. She wanted to offer him whatever comfort her idolizing presence might bring.

She stood before his door for a long time, an exterior of poise concealing the nervousness that grew steadily within her. He had to be there, she thought with growing agitation. And he wouldn't reject her because he was kind, even to strangers.

The door swung slowly open, shedding dim light from the tiny apartment. Fear gripped her in her abdomen as she looked at him. Tonight he was different. A potent whiff of bourbon ex-plained why, but she didn't care. He was hurt; he was like a

7

majestic animal brought down by the single, unexpected bullet of a beguiling but devious hunter. If he chose to drown his sorrows in the privacy of his own home, she understood.

He wore a terry bathrobe, and she stared at him for some minutes, convulsively swallowing, never having seen him before in such a state of near nakedness. She was acutely aware of and fascinated by the breadth of his golden-haired chest, displayed in muscled splendor by the loose V-neck of his robe. His legs beneath the ragged hem were as solid as shapely granite, thick with the same golden hair.

His eyes were bluer than cobalt, shocking with gem-studded brilliance, their intensity magnified because they were slightly red-rimmed. His face appeared more gaunt than usual, his cheekbones hollow. His thin nose with its exciting edge of arrogance was pinched. The firm line of his rugged jaw was blurred by a stubble of dark gold hair the same gold as those thick waves upon his head—a gold that she thought of as a halo surrounding him. A shining aura of invincibility. He was the epitome of all things good.

His bleary eyes blinked as he stared at her with equal evaluation, a mixture of emotions registering through the numbing fog of his mind.

He was surprised that she was there. He was stunned that he had never realized before how exotically lovely and exciting she was. He was curious, and also touched.

"What are you doing here?" he asked not unkindly, annoyed at the slur in his voice. He had been drinking, but hell, not that much.

"I—" She faltered only a second. "I came to see you. I knew you weren't going to the cast party. I, uh, I heard a few rumors about what happened and I thought you could use some company."

A slow, wry grin of rueful self-mockery broke across his face. "I'm not at the cast party to avoid company," he said bluntly, relenting immediately as he saw the crestfallen look upon her face that all the sophistication of her dress could not hide. "I didn't want to inflict my mood—or my rotten temper—upon

8

anyone else." His smile became twinged with a hint of tenderness. He knew she hero-worshipped him, which was soothing to his very bruised ego. And in his indolent way he cared for her. She was like a breath of fresh air. So honest, so innocently sweet . . . so different.

She smiled tentatively in return. "I don't believe your temper is all that rotten! I don't believe anything about you could be rotten!" she declared passionately.

Chuckling at her fervent surge of blind loyalty, he threw open the door. "Come in," he offered with a half-hearted shrug. Then bowing gallantly he added, "If I am to have company, I can think of none more preferable to yours. Have a drink with me."

She took a hesitant step into the small studio apartment. "Sorry about the mess," he murmured behind her back.

The place wasn't really a mess. Evidence of a customary fastidiousness could be seen in the cleanliness of the sparkling kitchen in the rear; only the bedroom/sitting room combination was in disorder. The Castro convertible was opened, and the sheets were crinkled as if he had just gotten up. A bottle of Wild Turkey sat open on an end table; an ashtray overflowed with cigarette butts. His clothing was strewn over the one fanback wicker chair, over the foot of the bed, and in a heap on the hardwood floor.

"What would you like?"

"Pardon?" She had been about to sit in the chair, but his voice, near to her ear as he silently padded behind her on bare feet, caused her to jump back up.

"A drink," he explained with patient amusement. "What would you like? I'm afraid the choice isn't a big one—bourbon, beer, or wine."

"Oh—ah—wine, please," she murmured, suddenly chilled by his haphazard swagger and the depth of pain in his eyes that his careless chivalry didn't quite hide.

"White wine," he muttered dramatically, repeating the words in a different tone as he walked to the refrigerator. "White wine. Ah, yes, suitable. White wine for the lady, a bourbon for myself." He laughed dryly. "Correction. Another bourbon for myself."

9

He made an elegant display of handing her a glass of the clear white wine, then picked up the bourbon bottle, drawing from it in a long swallow that caused him to wince. He wasn't drunk—not stinking drunk at any rate, but the warm numbing effect of the liquor on his savagely tormented mind was an anesthetic he couldn't resist.

And suddenly, so was she.

"Why aren't *you* at the party?" he demanded, seating himself at the foot of the bed and patting the space beside him.

She watched him warily, chewing her lower lip.

"Come over here!" He laughed and growled at the same time. "I'm not the big bad wolf. I don't bite. I nibble now and then." He teased her with wriggling brows. "But bite—never! Come on over and tell an older man why you're not at the party."

This was why she had come, she reminded herself—to be near him, to talk to him, to shiver at his touch, to take whatever crumbs fell her way. . . . But he wasn't the man she had adored from afar tonight. The man who could discuss the world with intelligence and wit. The man who never patronized. The man who could combine pride and dignity with compassion and kindness.

No, he was more. He was vulnerable and he was allowing her to see his vulnerability. He became even more endearing by becoming human. But frightening still. Like a great wounded animal, he might strike out. . . . There was a ruthlessness about him tonight, a carelessness.

Rising with a jerky motion, she moved over to him, smiling hesitantly. "I guess I just wasn't in the 'party' mood!" she said lightly, moistening her dry lips with the tip of her tongue. He watched her and she had no idea how fascinating he found the small motion.

"No, huh?"

"No!" Meeting his gaze with a bold surge of passionate emotion rising in her voice, she declared, "I heard, and well, damn! *She* shouldn't have gone to the party. You shouldn't have had to stay away!"

He clinked the bottle to her glass. "Bravo! I'm a lucky man

to have such a fervent fan!" His eyes gentled and he mused, "You are sweet. So sweet I wonder if you can be for real?" Chuckling in earnest, he touched the soft silky skin of her cheek. "I didn't go, beautiful sweet thing, of my own choice. I didn't want to be responsible for a murder. All females are not sugar and spice, and definitely not all things nice! Some are cunning witches of deceit."

"Lenore," she whispered, afraid to say the name, afraid to breathe lest he quit the touch of his callused yet gentle fingers upon her face.

He smiled bitterly, but continued his caress, his eyes on his thumb as its roughness grazed across her lips. He appeared to be deep in thought, but irresistibly intrigued by the movement.

"Yes, Lenore. You have heard the story. I was offered *the* big break. A call from Hollywood, a legit call. And lucky, lucky me. Lenore gets the call. And as fate would have it, dear, dear Lenore 'forgot' to give me the message. And now it's too late."

"Call them back!" she cried out, outraged.

"I did call back. But I was a very small fish being given a chance. I didn't move fast enough, and they hired another guy." He flung himself back on the bed, closing his eyes. "And what does the lovely Lenore have to say being caught in the act?" He shook his head vigorously in bewilderment with his eyes still closed. "She couldn't bear to see me go! Nice, huh? Especially if you know Lenore. She'd sell her own mother for a Broadway audition! Dear, lovely Lenore! What she couldn't bear was the thought of my having received an offer and not her!" Jerking back to a sitting position, he drained the remaining amber liquid in the bottle and hurtled it viciously across the room where it crashed with a deafening shatter against the white enamel refrigerator.

The girl gasped out a startled scream, shivering at the grim expression that held his jaw in a rigid line as well as from the shocking sound of the explosion. He looked at her as if suddenly remembering that she was there, a grimacing remorse unlocking his frozen face. "Sorry," he murmured with a sincere regret that was as quick as his flare of temper. He felt as if he had shot a

11

cannon over the head of a peacefully grazing doe. Smiling to ease the horror in her eyes, he laughed lightly and joked. "Anyway, you can see for yourself why I'm not at the party. I really hate acting like a bastard, I just guess that now and then none of us can help it. I prefer to be a bastard alone. Give myself a little time to get in control."

"Should I leave?" she queried softly.

"No." He really didn't want her to leave. She was having a soothing effect on him, drugging his pain with far more potency than the liquor. "No, don't leave."

"I'm sorry about Hollywood," she said compassionately.

"It's okay, kid, forget it." He smiled again with a more natural cheerfulness. "I will. By tomorrow I'll have forgotten all about it. I'll be able to chalk it all up to fate and keep on plugging." He looked at her deeply, his cobalt gaze growing more intent. "How old are you anyway?"

"Twenty-four," she lied mechanically, giving herself a few years because she knew he would consider her too young for him. "I'm going to head back to Florida State in the fall for my masters."

"I guess you're not such a kid," he whispered as his gaze slipped from her expertly made-up face to the pleasing curves beneath the silky sheath. He stood abruptly. "I owe you something for facing the bear. How about a Chinese dinner? Hoy Toy's delivers. I'd take you somewhere nice, but"—he gave her a devilish grin—"I'm really not up to getting dressed again."

"You don't owe me anything," she said proudly, her delicate chin rising. "I came here because I wanted to."

His hand rested on the top of her head, feeling the luster of the raven hair. With one finger he touched her uplifted chin. "Okay, I don't owe you anything. But how about dinner? Because I'd love to have you join me."

Her lips curled into a radiant smile. "I love Chinese food," she ventured shyly.

"Good," he chuckled. "We seem to have a lot in common." He didn't really have any devious plans, but he was allowing his fogged mind to rationalize as he never would under normal circumstances. She had come to him, she was certainly of age, she was stunningly, intoxicatingly sweet. . . .

He was gallant while they ate, entertaining her with tales from his days in the service and at Florida State. He kept her wineglass full, and continued to drink heavily, convinced he could hold his liquor. And he could, physically.

She was gratified, thrilled, and uniquely happy because he was happy. He was laughing again. He had forgotten the foul trick played upon him that had ruined his chance at stardom. And all because of her. She had done it. She had created his wonderful metamorphosis back to the gracious charmer whom she loved. The tender, satisfying sensation was overwhelming. She felt every inch a woman, totally feminine, and divinely powerful. The power was wonderful. Their knees touched beneath the small table, and as they would talk, his foot would tease along her calf, making her incredibly dizzy. She knew his every breath, each nuance, each movement. Lovingly she absorbed him, fascinated by the subtle things—the thin blue veins in his long, tanned hands; the short, clipped nails; the half curl of his lips as he spoke; the thatch of golden hair falling over one eye. The wonderful way his features split into charming lines as the blue eyes sparked into dazzling laughter. It was young love, her first love, a special love offered completely, without guile. Never would she be as acutely aware as she was this night, as sensitive to each new beauty.

And she knew that he watched her, his attraction growing as she was sure he began to realize how very much he cared for her too. All he had needed was this night, this wonderful, magical night to see her as the woman she was.

She was a better actress than she knew. Her touch, her words, her sensuous, sultry eyes . . . Yes, he saw her as a woman, one who knew exactly what she was doing.

But as all lovers fantasize, she was easily able to imagine at that moment that he loved her, only her, with the same fervor that came from her tender, young heart. The mood was drawn; it was more beautiful than anything she had ever known. They were an island that night, so very, very absorbed. The surround-

13

ings of the cheap efficiency apartment were nonexistent; they might have been in a castle of her fairy-tale dream-making. The boxed Chinese food might have been the most elegant of gourmet meals. And the rumpled cotton sheets on the bed might have been sheerest silk.

It was the most natural thing in the world for both of them to carry their wineglasses to that bed, to lay back together, and to talk, casually beginning to touch, to tease. It never occurred to her that his mind might be hazy, or that her own was far from lucid. The wine had been magnificent. It had stripped her of her shyness; it had numbed her inhibitions. When he touched her hair, she touched his, pushing that straying lock back over his forehead, marveling at the feel of it. It was thick, unruly, healthy-clean. It had the virile scent of him, so totally male. A scent that stayed on her flesh when he finally kissed her, that permeated her lips. A scent so deliciously him that she would remember it forever.

She was light, on a cloud, floating in an endless sea of mist, but poignantly aware of every sensation—the feel of his tongue plundering her mouth, that of perfect, hard white teeth scraping against hers in demand, filling her with innocent awe. The all-inducing touch of his mouth—alive, vibrant—moved with a sensuous command that electrified as it enmeshed her as surely as quicksand into a world that was totally him, totally sensuous. An unprotesting world of increasing joy. She didn't know what she was doing; she never bothered to think or worry. She just responded to his leads, unskilled, but achingly receptive. His kisses moved down the length of her throat; his hands sought her breasts beneath the silk, his fingers searching out the rim of her bra to rub her firm young nipples until they rose in jutting peaks.

And for him that wasn't enough. The soothing comfort she had brought him flash-fired into intense heat. He simply discovered her exquisite desirability. Longing constricted inside him with a primitive agony. Under no circumstances could he have thought rationally, and he wasn't going to try now.

He was knowledgeable; he was innately a tender if demanding lover. He divested her of the silk dress with seductive expertise,

14

slowly sliding it from her shoulders, allowing it to shimmer as it fell along her skin. There was nothing hurried to his actions; he was crystallized into enchantment as he uncovered the purity of her beauty. He didn't consciously think; he didn't plan. He savored this exotic gift from the heavens unquestioningly. His mind was whirling in heady, undeniable sensation.

She was in his arms when sure fingers found the single hook that held her blue lace bra. He discarded the garment without a fumble, his lips finding the mounds of pure sweet cream that trembled for his touch, arched with youthful pride. She whimpered as his tongue flicked lightly over her nipples; she cried aloud when his mouth moved over them heatedly tasting, then suckling with rough demand. Her fingers dug furiously into his blond hair.

It was as if a switch had suddenly been turned on. Her body was illuminated, filled instantly with a light of blue fire. A bittersweet mixture of unknown ecstasy and gnawing pain radiated from deep within the core of her lower abdomen to enflame throughout her with the wildness of a brush fire. She was amazed, delirious, stunned, and then incredibly lost, aware only of her drive to have more of him, for him to fill the wonderful, aching void that this beautiful new experience was evoking. There was craving, wanting, needing, desperate needing. All else was obliterated.

Her fingers were clamped so tightly in his hair that he had to release them gently before shifting to roll her stockings from her legs and fit his own fingers into the elastic strings that held her bikini panties. Even her feet were beguiling—small, smooth, the toenails glazed in a delicate pink. He kissed each one. . . .

Rising in sudden haste, no longer able to control the terrible urgency to have her, he threw his robe aside, watching her face, dimly aware that she had blanched, and that her eyes were wide, dilated. He eased his length upon her, shuddering with new, torturous delight as naked flesh met naked flesh. Holding her face, he kissed her again, drawing from her lips as a bee seeking nectar. Her arms wound slowly around his neck, and she clung to him, demanding that the torrid kiss be plundered to its depths.

His hands left her face; they savored strongly the slender curves of her body to her hips where they clamped firmly. His weight pinioned her, his hips and thighs upon her until his knee opened the final barriers to sweet consumption.

It was as he probed for that access that she was thunderstruck with a horrible moment of lucidity. The truth, the seriousness, of what she was doing came stridently home to her.

"Wait . . ." she breathed, twisting and writhing in unwitting assistance. "Please! Wait . . . stop. . . ." she wailed, bringing balled fists against the golden expanse of his chest. The effort was pathetic, as useless as her attempt to grip her fingers into the rock-hard biceps that pinned her to the bed. "Wait!"

He was not a cruel man, nor had he ever been in any way forceful. But his need for her now was as deep and fervent as the despair she had driven from him. She would have been pleased to know that he had never wanted a woman before with such an undeniable urgency. He simply wasn't in his right mind. He wasn't even filled with delusion. His mind, in fact, had nothing to do with it at all.

"You little tease!" he uttered harshly, the memory of another betrayal at the hands of a woman erupting inside him. His blue eyes burned with a fire that was deadly heat and frigid ice. "Too late to back out now, lady temptress, way too late."

And it was. He was young, he was virile; his desire throbbed against her with a tortured fever that commanded all else— seeking, finding, penetrating.

She fought him furiously for brief seconds of wild, shooting pain. Then she lay still, shocked.

He very dimly knew what he had done, but the thought was far from his consciousness. Nothing but culmination and her surrender could quench the delicious hunger of the raging passion she had elicited. Yet as she went pliant, he found a certain control and brought his demands from a hectic to a fluid rhythm, cajoling with each stroke, determined to please as he was pleased. He lulled her with his hands, with soft, soothing whispers. Slowly, slowly, he brought her back to him.

The pain receded; the glowing heat of that wild, craving desire usurping discomfort until it ebbed away entirely. She was swept into his wooing rhythm, gradually becoming as voraciously thirsting as he, demanding in return, greedily arching to claim his every thrust.

Her protests had been so ridiculous. There had never been such wondrous, awe-inspiring, shuddering bliss. She could spend her life in his arms, drowning, dying, loving, giving in this divine ecstasy. And he was hers. Completely. Never could two people come together like this—this closely, this thoroughly—without becoming one, without tenderly giving of their hearts. She had him in the oldest way known to woman. She could never belong to anyone else, never, never, and neither could he.

Thoughts of love stopped. He had brought her so high, so high that she could barely breathe. Every nerve, every movement, every fiber of her being—sight, sound, feeling—all were devoted to the frantic crescendo of the exquisite symphony his masterful rhythm had created. She was crying his name, shuddering convulsively, holding him, needing him, bursting into a brilliant white glory of sensation so beautiful it could never be imagined, only lived. He guided her through that mindless pleasure, groaning himself with the tremendous satiation of the devilishly sweet intensity of their mating.

He smiled at her with a mingling of tenderness and something that might have been surprise. Then, amazingly, he rolled from her, dead weight. She lifted the arm that still cradled her midriff. It fell to his side with a flop. His energy expended, his physical needs gratified to ultimate contentment, he had fallen asleep, simply passed out.

Tears of happiness hovered on her eyes as she watched him with a loving emotion that rose from and filled her breast. Her lips curved into a gentle smile. Even the wine she had consumed could not make her sleep; she was too riddled with wonder and excitement. She lay beside him, oblivious to time, softly stroking the lines of his magnificently sculpted back, positive that heaven itself could offer no greater reward than that of being loved by this man. She was giddy, smug with her love, satisfied, and fulfilled. She had truly become a woman in his arms. He cherished her.

He twisted suddenly in his sleep, reaching for her to nestle comfortably to his form. He mumbled drowsily.

Puzzled, she leaned closer to his lips, rubbing her soft cheek against his shadowed rough one. "What, my love?" she whispered with all the newfound joy and tenderness of their union. "What?"

"Love you," he murmured, and she ached with the bliss of his words. But he twisted restlessly and kept speaking as he stroked her with an absent hand. "Love you, Lenore." His hand stopped, and he flopped back into a sound, stuporous sleep.

Lenore? Lenore? The name blazed across her mind like a skull-splitting blow. She was stunned, too stunned for a moment to assimilate the awful agony. Then it rained down upon her like the icy dagger thrusts of a hailstorm. She was mortified, crushed; she would have happily and simply died. Her naivete was washed cleanly and completely from her mind. He didn't really care for her at all; she had deceived herself with a pathetic false confidence and a longing to make real what wasn't. She should have known. If he was in love with anyone, it was the lost Lenore, no matter what she had done.

But she—blind, innocent idiot that she was—had literally thrown herself at him and gotten exactly what she deserved. God, why was it all so clear with hindsight? How could she have been such a foolish dreamer just a few short hours ago . . . a few short minutes ago. . . .

With tears streaming down her face she rose and dressed in silence. The truth had been a cold, cruel, vicious slap in the face. She would never be the same. The night had aged her in a way that years never could. Seconds of harsh reality had really made her a woman.

Grabbing her handbag, she tiptoed unnecessarily to the door, but paused with perplexity as she noticed the telltale sheets. She slipped into her heels and began the mental process which would eventually become a shield over her heart. She wiped her stained cheeks and sighed over the loss of innocence and dreams and

18

withdrew to the safety of being frozen and numb. The pain would come to her again—she had yet to know how viciously—but now she had to think. She would have to face him again.

She looked dispassionately at his rugged features, at his golden hair, at his beautiful body. He would remember tonight, but what would he remember? A brief span of physical respite. A night like so many others he had experienced. A night that meant nothing. He would have to think it had meant absolutely nothing to her too. She would never allow him to humiliate her again. All he could offer was kindness and compassion—and maybe a coldblooded bodily desire, none of which she wanted from him.

She'd be damned if she'd have him know he had taken from her the most precious gift a woman could offer. He could wonder, but she would deny for an eternity that he had taken her virginity. He could think he was crazy. That would be preferable.

Grunting as she strained with all her strength to pull his muscle-bound weight about, she managed to strip the bed. He would have a good hangover in the morning and he deserved to wonder what the hell he had done with the sheets!

Nervously she rolled the sheets into a ball, doubting he could possibly awaken, but watching him warily nevertheless. She turned from him, her tears dried. She did not look back, and she did not cry again.

He awoke with the most godawful hangover he had ever had in his life. His head pounded with the ferocity of a thousand steel bands. His tongue felt dry and raspy, as if it had swollen to twice its normal size. Far worse than his physical pain was the ache and self-chastisement of memory. He reached for her, but she was gone. What had he done? He frowned, wincing as the motion increased the pounding in his head. Damn, it was all so vague. A mixture of beauty, of sweetness, of remorse. She had come to him, yes, but she was young, and he knew better.

No matter how delectable the fruit. No matter how tempting the offer. He knew the girl he had taken, and she had deserved so much more. So much more than a drunken bum wallowing

19

in self-pity. In all of his twenty-nine years, he had never felt a greater sense of shame. He was going to have to find her, to make it up to her.

His frown softened as a smile curved his lips. It wouldn't be hard. The memory of exquisite beauty and sweet ecstasy lingered along with the shame of his behavior. She wasn't so terribly young. Many another man would have thought her quite ripe and mature . . . and now it seemed as if he would be around for a while. Maybe something precious had been right under his nose all along. . . .

He groaned as he shifted on the bed, suddenly realizing that he had slept on a bare mattress. God, what *had* happened? What had he done? Pain blazoned through him again. He couldn't remember if she had come to him completely willingly, or if . . . He couldn't bear the thought, nor was he really sure. He remembered a piece of a rare heaven, so good, so shatteringly exciting that only a woman of experience should have been able to create it. But he had been so sure of her innocence, of her guileless honesty. Hell, he wasn't going to solve any riddles today. He would seek her out, but not today. Today he was going to have to learn to live with himself again. He swore to make a thousand tomorrows sweet for her. He closed his eyes with determination, remorse, and a strange wonder. But even closing his eyes hurt.

The phone rang. He almost didn't answer it. But he did, groggily, and snapped to attention when he heard his agent's voice. Then his head began to swim with the glittering future he thought he had lost.

In his last days at the theater, she knew that he watched her, she knew that he tried to see her. She avoided him as she would the plague, but did it with a very careful nonchalance. And when he finally caught her on his last day in town, she was as cool as a mountain stream. She pretended to be hiding annoyance when he called her name.

"About the other night—" He began catching her arm.

"What about it?"

20

The boredom in her drawl set him back.

"I—uh—I wanted to apologize. I wanted to see—" He was going to say "you again," but her brittle chuckle cut him off.

"Apologize? Whatever for? We're both adults." She shrugged with indifference. "It was nothing."

"Wait a—"

"I'm sorry," she smiled, pulling her arm away. "I can't wait. I have a date waiting for me."

He released her immediately, stunned and perplexed. "Good-bye then."

"Good-bye," she turned airily, and clipped her heels briskly across the floor.

But she couldn't leave it at that. She had to turn around. She would probably never see him again, unless it was on a television screen, or in one of those fan magazines.

"Hey!" she called cheerily. He looked at her with the hard blue stare that was about to become famous.

"Good luck!" she called with a thumbs-up sign. "Break a leg in Hollywood!"

"Thanks."

He watched her as she walked away, deciding he was no judge of human character. He didn't mean a damn thing to her! Women were a mystery, he thought with a dry chuckle. But one day . . . he'd like to see that little raven-haired vixen again. Now he could go on to his new life with a clear conscience.

He whistled happily as he left the theater. All his memories could be good ones.

CHAPTER ONE

"All right, let's call it quits for today."

Vickie closed her script and yawned. First readings were seldom very exciting, especially when the play was Shakespeare's *Othello*, which she knew like the back of her hand, as she had used it for the basis of her senior thesis back at FSU. Running her expressive gray eyes over the rest of the cast, she decided that no one had been particularly up for any real work today. Her fellow thespians were also yawning, stretching, and fumbling with their gear.

The same voice growled, "Get with it by tonight, guys!"

Vickie gave her director, Monte Clayton, a guilty smile. They were all acting like a group of disgruntled first-year drama students. Monte Clayton's Dinner Theatre was one of the finest in the eastern United States, possibly even the country. They were not a star-oriented ensemble, but a troop of dedicated, hand-picked actors and actresses who had worked together day and night for years. They constantly strove to bring their best work to a public long attuned to knowing that an evening at Monte's was well worth the price of the ticket—the food and performances were consistently excellent.

Vickie glanced at her wristwatch, surprised to see that they had broken up early. She was not due to pick Mark up from nursery school for almost two hours. Grinning, she decided to badger Monte for a while to see if he would give in and tell her the name of their mystery guest artist who would be playing Othello to her Desdemona.

Monte often gave in to her. She was only dimly aware that she was his most respected and admired actress, and that that was the reason. Whatever homage was paid her she accepted with a quiet grace that also made her a personal favorite of the other cast members. Despite the fact that she was a private person and seldom aired her own problems, she was the one to whom the others brought their day-to-day troubles.

Amidst friendly calls of "See ya later," and "Catch ya tonight," Vickie flung her bag over her shoulder and moved toward the stage, where Monte was scribbling ideas that had come to him during the reading. He looked up with surprise as Vickie approached him, and his eyes narrowed with a wary twinkle. On a cheerfully firm note he remarked, "You can stop right there, Miss Victoria Langley. I see that shade of feminine connivery in in your eyes, and I am not giving you a hint about our guest artist until I make the announcement tonight to the entire cast."

"Monte!" Vickie declared in a hurt tone. "I'm not here to pry! I have some extra time, and I thought you might buy me a cup of coffee."

Monte gazed at her sternly for a moment before releasing a resigned sigh. "Sure, love!" he chuckled. "I wish I could believe you were after the pleasure of my company. But that's okay, I like you trying to cajole me, even if the motives are devious." Rising with a sprightly jump, he pointed to a front row table. "Have a seat, Vick. I'll go 'buy' the coffee."

Vickie smiled, headed for the table and tossed her bag on one chair while sliding into the other. She opened her script and glanced idly over it, then tossed it on top of her bag. She would have her lines down pat within the next few days, wanting to have the tediousness of that chore out of the way early so that she could concentrate on the character. At the moment though, she was in no great hurry. Glancing around the room with tender affection, she scanned the hundred silent tables and the darkened stage presently set for the evening's performance of *Godspell*. She had been with Monte for two years now—two good years that had given her a pleasant and comfortable livelihood and kept her happy and eternally busy. She had little time for anything but the theater and her toddler son, Mark, and that was the way she wanted it. Her social life extended to her family and friendships with the other troop members, and that was the way she wanted it. She really had no time for men, which was fine with her.

She grinned, thinking of the group's nickname for her—Ice Maiden. Like many a performer, Vickie was shy offstage, and, admittedly, just not interested in any serious dating. She enjoyed friendly outings with an occasional admirer who pursued her, but having been burned once, she was too wise to get involved with any man. Victoria Langley, illustrious leading lady of the theater, was still basically Vickie Dalton of the small town of Bradenton. She had never grown bitter, but she had developed a frame of hard steel.

Without warning, her glance around the room brought back one unpleasant memory, one so well-buried she was shocked that it had entered her mind. *Foolish!* she admonished herself, and yet a feeling of uneasiness persisted. Annoyed, she calmly reminded herself that what had been, was done, finished; it had no bearing on the present or future. Life always went on, and for her it went on well.

"Why the sad eyes?" Monte demanded as he returned with two cups of steaming black coffee. Setting them down, he swung a wiry leg over a chair and joined her.

"Sad?" she repeated, focusing luminous gray eyes on him, then switching back to a smile. "I'm not sad at all. I was just thinking about this place and all it has done for me."

Monte's thin features broke into a wide grin. "When I look at you now, it is hard to remember that when I first met you, you were nothing but a gangly no-account kid hanging around the stage doors." His grin slipped a little. Vickie had been one of the numerous college kids who always came his way, willing to do anything to slip a foot into the door of a professional theater.

He hadn't thought much of her, just another young girl, all saucer eyes and dark black hair, who disappeared at the end of a summer season. Then, a year later, he had discovered her again, playing a tear-jerking and incredible Juliet on a Charleston stage. After the play he found her backstage and immediately offered her a permanent, well-paying job with him, no questions asked.

The skinny kid had matured into a brilliant and hard-working actress, now shapely with a mane of long, gleaming hair. She wasn't exactly beautiful; her nose was a trifle too tilted, and the gray eyes, with thick inky black lashes, were still too big for her fragile bone structure. But she arrested one's attention with sheer vivacity. Many a greater beauty could sit in a room, but all eyes would turn to Victoria, and hearts would thud at her soft-spoken, gracious manner. Like my own! Monte thought wistfully. He, the cool director, had fallen head over heels in love with her, only to be crushed when she nicely informed him that if he had anything in mind other than a professional relationship, she would leave.

Swallowing his ego, pride, and desire, he had insisted she stay. The years had proved him wise. Unwilling to give her love, Vickie gave him her tireless energy. She expended her multifaceted resources faultlessly for the theater and him, pitching in with a good-natured cheer to help in any circumstance. She earned the regard of the crew and the restaurant employees as well as the cast—building, painting, sewing costumes, and cleaning tables if needed—a sterling example for anyone associated with Monte's. Although it was clear she would never be his wife or lover, she was his friend, a valued one.

Vickie widened her smile and remarked, "I *was* such a stage-struck kid! And I grew up lucky. I got to live my dreams. I remember. . . ." Her voice trailed off suddenly as that unbidden memory replaced the one she had been about to relate. Damn! she told herself, thoroughly disgusted and annoyed. What was the matter with her today? Taking a sip of her coffee and lowering murky lashes over her eyes to hide them, she determinedly pushed the discomfort back where it belonged—out of her mind!

"Remember what?" Monte asked, eyeing her quizzically.

"Oh, nothing. Well, lots of things, really!" She resolutely laughed. "Remember when we did *The Heiress* and Patty Shaffer lost her contact lens in the tea set?"

Monte threw back his graying head and practically roared

with laughter. "Unfortunately I do! How about the night Harry Blackwell was making his dramatic exit in *Blood Wedding* and the door fell in on him?"

As they chuckled over each disastrous absurdity, Vickie totally forgot her uneasiness. Her natural exuberance brushed it aside, and she felt smug with her life. It was a good one, and she loved it. She even forgot her original reason for cornering Monte as they talked. Finally she realized she had fiddled away far more time than she had intended, and unless she got going, she would be late in picking up Mark. Jumping hastily to her feet, she wailed, "Darn your hide, Monte. I had meant to cajole that name from you, and you made me forget all about it. Now I have to go!" She gave him a beseeching look, arching her brows. "Come on, Monte, how about giving me a clue at least?"

"No way!" he responded with a firm grin. "Not this time. You are going to be enthralled along with everyone else!"

"Turkey!" she snorted teasingly. "Okay," she sighed in a martyrlike tone. "Make me suffer!"

"It won't be for long," Monte promised. "I'll tell you everything after tonight's show. Might as well"—he shrugged—"he'll be here tomorrow."

"Just as you say, boss man, see you tonight!" Vickie swung her bag over her shoulder, grabbed her script, and kissed his weathered cheek.

"I'm glad to hear you remember I'm the boss!" he chuckled gruffly.

Wrinkling her nose at him, Vickie waved and walked out the doors, blinking beneath the glare of the blinding sunlight. It was going to be a hot summer. It wasn't the first of June yet, and already they were hitting temperature readings in the nineties. But she was a Floridian, accustomed to the heat, and an avid fan of the endless white beaches of her native state—a happy, often barefoot waif on the sands.

Settling into the driver's seat of her sturdy old Volvo, she hummed a tune for the night's show. *Godspell* was fun to do. She would be sorry when its run ended, although she truly loved to do Shakespeare, especially with a director like Monte. He

26

brought so much to a play, listening to and respecting the opinions of his players. Of course, though, his word was final.

Parking outside her son's small nursery school, she waited only seconds before she saw Mark coming out with his teacher. Her heart took another unexpected lurch as he looked for her, found her, waved, and with his beautiful lopsided grin, ambled to the car. She had been lucky in a way. Mark was the spitting image of her. Except for two things—his eyes were brilliant blue like his father's, and he had the same killer grin.

"Mum!" he chortled happily as Vickie buckled him into his car seat and waved an okay sign to the wary teacher who made sure her charge was safely in his mother's hands.

"How was your day, my darling?" Vickie crooned, kissing his raven head. "What did you do?"

"Play," Mark said happily. "Play."

Vickie chuckled. He was only twenty-seven months old—not much of a conversationalist. But he grinned happily when she suggested ice cream.

Over gooey fudge sundaes, they shared precious time together. Vickie's only remorse over her chosen career was it took so much time away from Mark. Although Monte's was "dark" on Sundays and Mondays, the rest of the week was hectic. Vickie's daily schedule would cause a weaker person to wince; she dropped Mark off by eight at his school so that she could be at the theater by eight thirty, rehearsed the upcoming production until two, retrieved Mark by two thirty, and had to be back at the theater by seven to makeup and dress in costume for the current play. Those few hours in the afternoon she devoted to Mark.

Tousling his silky hair, she marveled at what a wonderful child he was. Shaking her head slightly, she wryly thought that blessings did often come in disguise. Mark had been such a blessing. Discovering her pregnancy had been the greatest trauma of her life, but his birth had brought her the most profound joy. He was more than her child now; he was her companion, critic, and friend.

"Finish your sundae," she directed him. "We'll scoot over to the beach for a bit."

"Beesh!" he repeated happily. "Beesh."

Sarasota, to Vickie, was the epitome of all that Florida should be. The city was quaint, clean, and bright beneath its year-round sun. Winters brought a mild snap of cold weather, never harsh, but just right for a subtle change of pace. Around November the population drastically increased as part-time residents, deserting the ice and snow of their northern habitats, ventured south. They helped to keep the city financially sound and also helped to fill the four hundred seats at Monte's.

Sitting on a patch of bleached sand while Mark played on the foam-flecked shore, Vickie luxuriated in the feel of the salt spray around her, her skin vibrantly attuned to its gentle caress, her toes tickled by the lapping touch of the encroaching tide. A fiddler crab sidled by her and disappeared into a small black hole as it sensed her movement. Smiling, she lay back on an elbow and grimacingly compared herself to the crab. She always disappeared at the slightest hint of danger. Maybe it was time for a change. Maybe she should become a little wilder, get out more.

"Hey, tiger." She softly called her entranced son. "We have to go now." At his crestfallen look she added, "We'll have burgers and french fries, okay?"

Vickie was never quite sure just how much her two-year-old understood, but "french fries" was as familiar as "beach" to him. He smiled again and she swept him up in her arms to head back to the car. "We have to hurry a bit, sweet pea," she murmured. "I have to have you all fed and set for bed before Mrs. Gilmore arrives. We don't want to lose her!"

She smiled at the thought. Harriet Gilmore, the plump matron who cared for Mark five nights a week, adored him. She probably wouldn't leave Vickie's employ even if she were beat over the head with a poker. A natural with children, the kindly lady loved Mark, and although Vickie knew she was prejudiced, she could understand why. Her son was blessed with a cheery disposition that seldom failed. He had never been a crier or whiner, and although he did have a temper tantrum now and then like any normal child, his basic nature was beguiling and endearing.

28

A charmer with a temper, Vickie thought a touch dryly. Like his father.

But, like his father, he usually displayed his temper only to himself. When a toy would frustrate him, he would flounce his sturdy little body into his room, where he would often stay despite her cajoling until he could emerge bubbling again.

At first Vickie had often attempted to deal with his moods. But as time and experience had taught her to control her own mixed feelings, she had accepted that he *was* like his father, and that that father had certain commendable traits that she should appreciate in her son.

Even at two Mark needed to deal with his problems in his own way. Vickie was wise enough now to simply be there when he decided that he needed her.

They drove into a sterile, fast-food restaurant, where Vickie bought hamburgers, french fries, and shakes. She didn't usually like to eat at burger places, and the strange uneasiness she had felt during the day seemed to stay with her, making her nervously lazy. She didn't believe in premonitions. She felt as if she should know something, *realize* something, but she couldn't put a finger on what it was she should know.

Well, one thing she did know, she told herself, was that she was going to get out more. She chuckled suddenly at that thought. She had had dinner a few times with last year's summer guest artist, and that had been a disaster. Monte always brought in a "star"; in doing so he could guarantee filling the house in the customary off season. Last year's "star" had been the popular hero of a motorcycle cop series—handsome and rugged on the screen, devoid of personality off. He had difficulty lifting a two-by-four in the shop and his egotistical immaturity drove Vickie to boredom.

Granted, she could remember being devastatingly immature just a few short years ago. But she had been naive. No, stupid was more like it! Okay, stupid, naive, overly sheltered—a pathetic twenty-two. And now an ancient twenty-five.

It wasn't really fair for her to judge anyone, her own mistakes had been so vast. One day she would have to explain to her son why he didn't have a father. Stop! she wailed to herself. Mental torture didn't solve anything. This was a hell of a time to worry about what she had long reconciled herself to anyway. Besides, the moral standards of the world had relaxed quite a bit. Mark would fare well, even if he never knew his father. But Mark could never know. No, Mr. Langley would have to stay dead. Better a dead loving parent than a living legend who would never recognize one's existence.

She was still worrying about the past later when she drove to the theater. "What is this? Drive-myself-buggy day?" she groaned furiously. She never did this to herself. Maturity had long since risen to squelch reproach as well as careless passion. Her decisions had all been made three years ago. It was all water over the dam.

Sliding onto her dressing-room stool, Vickie greeted the other four permanent female members of the troop as she switched on her mirror lights, listening and joining into their banter as she carefully began to apply her makeup base with a damp sponge.

"Vickie?"

She turned from her concentration to see Connie Weber calling her from the other side of the room. Connie was the troop's youngest member, a petite redhead, still struggling for confidence.

"Would you mind running through the song again before curtain?" Connie asked tentatively.

"Sure!" Vickie agreed, remembering her own days of stage fright with compassion. She and Connie harmonized on "Where Are You Going," a song Vickie considered to be the loveliest in the show despite the popularity of "Day by Day."

Painting a large red heart on her cheek, Vickie smiled. "I'll be with you in just a second." A few final touches completed her zany makeup and she was on her feet, slipping into her ragamuffin wig and heading for the door.

"I don't know why you're bothering," Terry Nicholson, a former New Yorker, jeered smugly. "She never gets it right."

"Terry!" Vickie admonished, surprised and wondering what had set off the venom from the tall, sophisticated brunette.

Maybe Terry was angry about *Othello*. She had been cast in a variety of small roles, mostly male, and she heartily resented the fact. But Monte tolerated no prima donnas—they were lacking males for the play and Terry was the most likely candidate to make up for the deficiency because of her height and throaty voice. Little Connie had been chosen for Bianca, the role Terry had wanted.

"Be nice!" Vickie said with a touch of amusement for the attractive friend she didn't quite trust. "Monte promised you Lady Macbeth for next year, and, besides, Connie has a beautiful voice. She just needs a little push!"

Terry grimaced dryly and sniffed. Shrugging, Vickie left her behind and hurried to the depths of the left stage wing to find Connie, peeking her head discreetly around the curtain to check out the size of the house.

It was full. Handsomely dressed customers sat at every table, some boisterous, some quiet, all eating with apparent pleasure. Vickie felt the small tug of excitement she always did before curtain, no matter what the play, no matter how long she had worked in the theater. Still, *Godspell* was special. The rolling repartee of the play worked well with their close-knit ensemble, drawing to the inevitable ending of the death of Christ with a poignancy that sent many an audience member off into the night teary-eyed and sniffling. Even atheists! Vickie thought, laughing to herself.

"Places—ten minutes!" The strict command of Jim Ellery, the stage manager, drew Vickie from her meanderings.

Hurrying back, she found Connie with Lara Hart at the practice piano. Lara, a fortyish woman of simple, quiet dignity, gave her a grateful smile. Monte's brilliant but often perplexed musical directress had been with him off and on since he had opened the place. All cast members had to be able to carry a tune, just as they had to know some rudiments of dance and mime, but they were not singers per se, a fact that sometimes left Lara sadly frustrated. "Thanks for rushing, Victoria," Lara said softly. "Connie does seem to do better when she's had a run through."

"I didn't rush!" Vickie assured her. "And I never mind rehearsing the song."

They worked on the song and Connie hit every note unfalteringly. What quality she has! Vickie thought with a touch of open envy. Her own voice was a pleasant alto, strong and melodious, but more from training than natural ability.

"Places!" Jim's order rang in their ears, and the cast scampered to the wings as the opening lights glittered in their colored gels.

"Slow down a bit on 'Turn Back Oh Man,'" Lara hissed in final instruction as Vickie nodded an okay and rushed along with the others.

"Curtain!" Jim commanded.

The magic of the theater began, stilling every noise in the audience of hundreds. Vickie forgot everything but the play, becoming an integral part of the wheel that made the fantasy on the stage live—singing, dancing, and giving a spontaneity to her lines that belied the fact she had already been saying them for four weeks.

"Good, up show!" Monte praised them as the curtain brought an end to act one. "Keep up that energy!"

"You sure are in a good mood," Vickie commented as he tweaked her heart-painted cheek in passing. "Not that I'm not, but you should let us in on the stars in your eyes!"

"One 'star.' Our guest is here." Monte smirked. "He came in a day early."

"He must have conjured up the spirit of Clark Gable!" Bobby Talford, the talented, homely actor playing the Christ role, said with a grimace. "I've never seen Monte this smug over a summer acquisition, and I've been here ten years!"

"Listen, smarty," Monte replied with good humor. "You, Mr. Talford, of all people, will be wiping that patronizing expression right off your face when you see who it is!" With that he folded his hands behind his back and walked away jauntily, knowing he had embedded new fits of curiosity.

"Me of all people," Bobby mused as they waited for the curtain to rise on act two. He looked at Vickie, his face scrunched in bewilderment.

"Hey, don't look at me!" she protested, laughing. "I haven't the faintest idea of who he is talking about. Have you had any crushes on any macho motormen lately?"

"Real cute, Victoria," Bobby retorted, lightly pulling one of her black pigtails. Shrugging his perplexity away, he continued. "I guess I don't have long to be curious, but Monte's secrecy has been driving me crazy!"

"Me too," Vickie admitted. "I even stayed today to try and trick him into telling me, but no go."

"Oh, we'll know in about an hour," Bobby whispered as they once more heard Jim calling "Places."

"Probably no big deal!" Vickie whispered back, moving to her spot in the wing. "Monte likes suspense."

Later that night she would wince in memory of her own words. But luckily she didn't know that now. Susan Morgan and Lynn Vale, the other two women rounding out the female side of the cast, entered into a tapped rendition of "Learn Your Lessons Well" and act two was on its way.

Toward the end of the show, a faint glimmer in the darkened audience caught Vickie's attention for a split-second. The muted light of a single candle had caught on a patch of blond hair. Odd, she thought. She hadn't noticed anyone with a truly golden head of hair in the audience when she had playfully run about flirting with her "Turn Back Oh Man" number. She dismissed the slight feeling of confusion. One of her cues was coming up. Then Christ was being crucified on the white picket fence, and it was time for the finale.

The curtain fell on act two only to reopen for the cast to take their bows to the sound of thunderous applause. They sang "Day by Day" again, and finally all ran off for the wings and their dressing rooms.

"Hey!" Jim caught them. "Forget changing for the moment. Monte wants you all out front and center in five minutes."

Grumbling slightly, they all meandered toward the stage.

33

"This better be good," Terry said with an exaggerated yawn. "I've got a date."

"We're meeting our mystery guest," Vickie told her, wishing that he hadn't arrived early. She was longing for the comfort of home and the cool, crisp sheets of her bed. The greasepaint on her face was beginning to itch and her two tightly drawn pigtails were becoming painful. "Cheer up," she advised the woebegone Terry dryly. "From what Monte says, we'll be so excited that a lost date will mean nothing to you."

"A lost date always means something to me," Terry retorted with a wince. "We're not all long-lost virgins, you know." She studied Vickie curiously for a moment as if seeing her for the first time. "I guess you can't be that though. I mean, Mark does exist. Whatever did happen to *Mr.* Langley?"

"Coffee anyone?"

Vickie glanced at Bobby with sheer gratitude for his timely arrival. "I'd love some!" she proclaimed. "In fact, you and Terry go sit—I'll get the coffee."

She hurried into the vast kitchen, exchanging friendly words with the waiters and waitresses she passed. Pouring three cups of coffee, she drew deep breaths before returning to the dining room now peopled only by the cast and a few scattered restaurant employees finishing up with their tables.

Why couldn't she just be blasé and tell the truth? There was no Mr. Langley, never had been, except in the telephone book, and her finger had simply fallen on the name.

She hadn't cared then, not about much of anything. Her mother, gently proving her love and her mettle, steered her on a course of action. "Victoria, your father and I can't force you to do anything. You won't tell us the name of the father, and I'm sure you have your reasons. But you want to keep your baby and I can't say that I blame you. I could have never given away a piece of myself either. But honey, let us help you! I know you think your life is over; it's not. For your own sake and that of the baby, go away for a year. Take on another name. Dad and I still want you to follow that dream, to make it as an actress."

There had been no recriminations, no harsh words, judgment,

or disappointment. And so emerged Mr. Langley, and a Victoria Langley who learned to appreciate the kindness and wisdom of her parents. She had the baby without ever breathing the truth of his paternity. After the birth she immediately auditioned for a South Carolina summer stock company and earned the role of Juliet. And it was there that Monte found her again on one of his talent-seeking trips, unable to believe that the girl had changed so drastically in a single year. Sometimes it amazed her that she seemed so terribly different from other young women her age. But then, she had had little to do in that year except wait and change, reconcile and mature.

"You know, Vick," Bobby said as she set the coffee before them and sat down. "You really are amazing. Thanks."

"Too good to be true," Terry interjected dryly.

"The beautiful green eyes of jealousy!" Bobby teased. He loved to irritate Terry. "Vickie, won't you reconsider and marry me? I'm really such a nice guy!"

Bobby asked her to marry him at least once a month. It was a standing joke between them. "Let me sweep you into my arms and take you away from all this," he continued dramatically. "I promise to make you forget all about the mysterious man in your past who holds your heart away from us all." He ended his comical speech by grabbing her hand and pressing his forehead into it.

"Bobby," Vickie moaned, "will you stop it? Monte is going to walk in any moment with our overly prized artist, and we'll look like a couple of idiots!" And besides, she thought, no one would ever make her really forget the man in her past. In three years she hadn't managed to forget him.

She had hated him enormously at times, but she knew there would never be another like him, never be another man who could send her to heaven with the slightest touch, command her love and respect with a single whisper, whose lean, tall frame could send shivers down her spine with mere memory.

"Where the heck is Monte?" Terry complained irritably. "If he doesn't show up soon, I'm leaving!"

As if on cue, Monte suddenly came striding out from the

35

darkened stage to sit at its edge, his legs dangling. "Sorry to have kept you all waiting. I should have let you get out of costume." He grinned delightedly. "Our guest was spotted by reporters and held up, but he'll be here momentarily."

"Who is it—God?" Terry muttered, unintentionally audible.

Monte gave her a sharp stare, and she had the grace and good sense to smile as if her words had been a joke. "Come to think of it, Miss Nicholson, I think you did compare him to God at one time," Monte said dryly, his grin taking on a slightly malicious cast. "A few of you know him, a few of you know only his work."

Monte's voice droned on, but Vickie wasn't listening anymore. Small stabs of fear were beginning to shoot through her. It couldn't be! No, it just couldn't be him, she thought desperately. The last she had heard, he had completed one of the recently popular space-adventure movies and gone on to Broadway. His television series had been successful, but he had pulled out when he felt its course had been run.

No! She shook her head vaguely, feeling the whip of her pigtails as they hit her face. How absurd. He had been gone three years. He was worth a fortune; he could call his own shots. Why should he come back to such a comparatively small theater town?

"Oh, and here he is now!" Monte said, jumping to his feet and smiling warmly toward the dark right wing from where Vickie could hear assured footsteps and just begin to see the tall, broad-shouldered frame of a man. "Ladies and gentlemen," Monte called in a ringing voice, "may I present with much pride and great pleasure one of my own protégés, our summer guest, Mr. Brant Wicker."

The room filled with ecstatic applause, but Vickie didn't hear it. A buzzing began in her ears as her face blanched beneath the greasepaint. She sat motionlessly, not able to register thought, as Brant appeared on the stage, his cobalt eyes twinkling merrily, his full, sensuous mouth set into a heart-rending grin, his blond head gleaming like a halo.

Then, as if she were an outside observer, an unknown entity

sailing above her own body, she made a few mental notes. He had changed. His jaw was squarer, firmer, his face leaner, the hollows beneath his high cheekbones more pronounced. Small lines etched their way around his eyes and the corners of his mouth. His body was still long and trim, wire-muscled, but it had filled out; the shoulders and chest were now wide, tapering to a narrow waist and slim hips.

Like a marionette, Vickie jerked around as Bobby emitted a loud yelp and rushed for the stage to pump Brant's hand. Terry followed him; they had been the two who had worked with Brant before, the two who had been with the company before Brant Wicker, the Tampa football hero turned actor, had left his home state for fame and fortune. A cacophony of excited voices rippled through the room, but they didn't register in Vickie's mind. Only the deadly buzzing. Nice guy, she thought, the words shooting shrilly in her mind. That was what even the most probing and vile of the fan magazines said. Oh, yeah, nice guy. Good man. Ethical, dignified, and unaffected. Hysteria was rising beneath her immobility. Calm down! she warned herself, finally managing to lick her parched lips. Play it cool! He won't remember, I know he won't remember.

Monte was walking with Brant around the tables where the cast sat scattered, introducing him to all the members. Vickie reached across the table for Bobby's pack of cigarettes and somehow lit one without fumbling. She seldom smoked—it was hard on a performer—but at the moment she needed that cigarette as much as she usually needed air to breathe. Inhale, exhale. "That's better," she told herself, noting thankfully that her long, slender fingers were steady and her hands composed.

"Come to think of it," Monte was telling Brant as they approached her, alone now at the table, "I think you have met Victoria. If I'm not mistaken, she was running around here your last summer." Directing his gaze to Vickie with a puzzled frown, he asked, "Wasn't that the summer you were here, Vick?"

"Yes," Vickie replied coolly, raising her eyes to meet the crystal blue stare of Brant Wicker. "Yes, Mr. Wicker and I have met. We were here the same summer." Forcing a stiff smile, she continued. "To be honest, I scarcely remember it myself, so I'm sure Mr. Wicker doesn't."

"Brant, please," their guest insisted, sliding his long frame into the chair beside Vickie's and studying her with an intense, contemplative assessment that made her throat burn dry. "Vickie. I remember you very well. I remember a very special night we shared, a night when I was really down and you pulled me back up by the hair."

Vickie shook her head and stretched her smile with an apologetic blankness. "Sorry, I don't remember that."

His brow raised teasingly. "Don't you?"

"No," she said flatly, coldly, dragging on her cigarette. "I'm afraid three years is a long time ago to me. I have problems remembering last week." She attempted to smile again and sprang to her feet. "Brant, it's a pleasure seeing you again. Monte, forgive me, but I have to get out of here. I can't keep Mrs. Gimball too long."

Vickie!" Monte protested. "I wanted you to have a drink with Brant and me. You two will be working very closely together. You could chat a bit, renew an old acquaintance."

If there was anything she didn't want to do, it was renew an old acquaintance. "Sorry, I have to go."

Her polite excuses might have been working on Monte, but they certainly weren't on Brant. He rose slowly and took her hand in a gentle but strong grip from which she couldn't possibly escape without making a scene. His jaw was hardened, and his blue eyes were narrowed dangerously. "Really, Miss Langley, do come along." His voice was steel-plated. "We'll be spending a lot of time together, you know." A warning rang beneath his pleasant words, one intended to be noted by her only, but she could read it plainly in his eyes. *I don't understand this, but I don't put up with petty grievances on stage.*

"I can't join you," Vickie snapped. "Excuse me."

As she moved toward the dressing room, she heard snatches of their conversation.

"I don't know what's gotten into Victoria," Monte said rueful-

38

ly. "She's usually the most pleasant person you'd ever want to meet."

"Who knows," Brant replied with an offhand shrug. "I believe I stepped on her toes three years ago. But she certainly did turn into a stunning young woman. . . ."

Vickie slammed the door to the dressing room and sank into her chair before she fell down. Her body had become as formless as wet cement, and she was shaking like a dry leaf in winter. This can't be happening, she thought, laughter bubbling in her dry throat. Not this nightmare!

But it was. Brant Wicker had returned. Tears were forming in the large gray eyes that returned her stare from the mirror. A summer! she moaned inwardly. An entire summer. I'll never make it. And what will happen when he sees Mark? Nothing, she assured herself, concentrating on long deep breaths for control. Nothing. No one could possibly see a resemblance. Just keep playing it cool and everything will be all right.

Without taking off her makeup she changed into her street clothing and fled from the theater. At home she thanked Mrs. Gimball and fell into bed as soon as the baby-sitter left. But Vickie couldn't sleep. The memory she had been fighting all day was upon her, flooding over her like the massive wash of a tidal wave. Her cheeks burned with a humiliation compounded rather than diminished by the years, and she tossed about her bed fitfully. The buzzing she had experienced earlier turned into a taunting monotony that whispered a name over and over and over . . . Brant Wicker . . . Brant Wicker . . . Brant Wicker . . .

CHAPTER TWO

Brant Wicker, at twenty-nine, had been everything a girl could want, a handsome daredevil, assured and confident, master of his own fate, aloof and yet courteous to a point of distraction. Those who had known him in his college days assumed he might head for pro-ball, law, or eventually politics. He followed none of the assumptions, enlisting in the service, and then arriving at Monte Clayton's Dinner Theatre.

Seldom had anyone seen such a natural for the stage. Within a year, about the same time a dewy-eyed Vickie fresh out of college became an apprentice with the group, Brant was taking all the leading roles, creating a host of ardent fans, male and female. He possessed just the right combination of macho toughness and compassionate down-to-earth reality to make women love him and men admire him.

Working with the group in her menial capacity, doing whatever needed to be done, Vickie admired and adored him from afar. To his credit, his ego was never inflated, and he was friendly with everyone from the lowest busboy to his employer, Monte. Vickie was touched by that kindness; she cherished it and built it into something else deep within her heart. Her fantasy of his secretly returning her feelings became a reality within the hidden recesses of her own mind. Dreaming—a fallacy and beauty of youth.

She had discovered, however, before that curious night of fate, that he was capable of being moody. Repairing a costume long after the theater had closed one night, she was surprised to hear noises from the stage. Tentatively she wandered from the costume shop to the dining room. Brant was sitting on the stage, dangling his legs and thumping them against the stage with distraction. His eyes were narrowed fiercely, his features tight in a scowl, his arms crossed in a vise over his chest. Suddenly, as she hesitantly wondered what to do, he looked up and noticed her partially hidden form. "Who's there?" he demanded sharply.

"Me," Vickie squeaked, cowering before the uncharacteristic wrath in his eyes.

"Me?" His impatient sarcasm was lightened by a touch of growing amusement. "Me who? Come down here. Let me see you."

Picking her way through the tables, Vickie complied with dread. She had never seen him angry before, and the fact that his anger seemed to be directed at her did nothing to still her pounding heart.

"Vickie, isn't it?" he inquired with a frown when she stood before him. "What are you doing here so late?"

She couldn't answer right away, her throat had constricted. The scent of his clean, crisp aftershave was assailing her, and she stared at the corded muscles in his arms, bared as his shirt sleeves were rolled high. A pulse beat in a blue vein that was just visible on his bicep, and she glued her eyes to it in fascination, fearing fancifully that if she were to look directly into his deep blue gaze, she would turn to salt.

"What are you doing here?"

His demand sounded in her ears again and she stuttered, "A-a costume. I was sewing a c-costume." Having found her voice, she found courage. "What are you doing here?"

"Brooding," he replied, blunt and brief. At the hurt look in her soulful gray eyes he softened. "Sorry, little girl, I shouldn't take this out on you." Sliding onto his side and resting his head on the hand of a crooked arm, he explained: "I had a bit of an argument with Monte, and I'm having to realize he was right. I'm cooling off so I can go apologize."

Nothing had registered in Vickie's mind except that her idol had called her a little girl. She had to set the record straight.

"I'm not a child," she exclaimed in indignant reply.

"No?"

41

"No, I'm a college graduate."

"Whew!" he whistled. "Forgive me!" The teasing twinkle she so loved was returning to his eyes. "You're a real old hag!"

Vickie blushed and lowered her head. "No, I'm not!" she murmured, raising her head to meet his eyes with a flash of defiance in her own. "But I'm also *not* a child."

"No?" His voice held a strange note as he raked his amused blue gaze down her body. "Maybe not, come here and we'll see."

Her feet seemed glued to the floor. His brows rose mockingly and she knew he still teased her even as he watched her speculatively. "What's the matter, little girl?" he chuckled.

That decided her. She had the vague suspicion that he was comparing her to the tempestuous Lenore she had heard he dated, and she was determined that he would find her to be far more worthy of his attentions than that siren. Tilting her head high, she moved slowly toward the stage, vaulting the edge with a graceful leap. She sat beside him, crossing her beautiful legs provocatively and looking deep into his eyes.

She could still the quivers that raced through her; she could hold her head high . . . be enticing. She was going to be an actress and could hide the fear that threatened to tug her from the stage and send her flying into the night.

He had meant to tease, to brush her lips, to promise solemnly she would be a beautiful woman one day before sending her on her way. But when his arms came around her, he found himself dragging her lengthwise beside him, claiming her lips in a caressing kiss which, begun as a joke, quickly became something else as a fire kindled in both of them—Brant, the man who had dated only mature women, his own age or older, women attuned to flirtations, and Vickie, the girl who so far knew little except the pursuit of elusive and hazy dreams. . . .

His weight shifted over hers; his powerful hands began a delightful exploration, slipping beneath the material of her blouse and searching her bare skin with tantalizing finesse. His thoughts meshed and mingled with his desires.

She was not that young; she was very much a woman. Her innocent response belied a deep sensuality, now budding beneath his practiced touch. Her flesh was alive, warm, beautiful, enticing.

But it was wrong. He had an understanding with Lenore, who thought no more of making love than she did of taking a walk. And somehow he knew this girl was different. Each experience for her would be special. She would give and take and cherish—and trust. He wasn't the man for her. She deserved a young man of her own, one who could give with total commitment before taking. He broke from her, his breathing harsh and ragged.

Vickie looked into his darkened eyes, confused. She had forgotten everything in the pleasure of his arms. Now his look was angry again, and all she knew was that she ached, painfully, mentally and physically. She didn't want to moralize; she simply longed to have him meld her body to his sinewed one once more, longed to understand and broaden the marvelous new sensations that he awakened to a rage within her. But he had withdrawn, irrevocably.

"What's wrong?" she asked hesitantly, suddenly feeling very awkward beneath his dark gaze.

"Nothing," he muttered hoarsely. He made a feeble attempt at one of his careless grins. "It's just that, well, you're right. You're not a little girl at all." Uncrossing his legs, he rose and reached a hand down to her. "Come on, Vickie, I'll take you home."

Vickie bolted up in her bed, shaken by her dreams. A feverish feeling had left her shivering; beads of perspiration had broken across her forehead. Hindsight was cruel, she thought, groaning aloud. How could she have been so pathetically naive?

She had been alone with Brant only twice—the one night at the theater, which had precipitated the second: her going to his house. Never had he instigated the dalliance. It had been she, fueling a fire with no regard for the consequences.

And now he was back, apparently with a surprising memory of what she thought he might have forgotten. It was doubtful that he remembered the stolen kiss of her waking dream—he had certainly shared a thousand such kisses. But he surely did remember the night she came to his house, and it was evident already he didn't intend to let her forget.

She had never really blamed him. Her decision to keep her secret a secret had been based on several factors, the main one complimentary to him. He might have wanted to marry her and she couldn't have, knowing that he cared nothing for her. Furthermore, his whole career was before him. He had become a success almost overnight. It would have been too ridiculous to put through a call to Hollywood and say, "Hey, Brant, we really don't know each other that well, but I'm the friend you consider to be a sweet little girl. Well, anyway, you know that night I said was nothing. I'm afraid there's something after all. . . ." Who in their right mind would have believed her?

No, what she had done had been for the best. Her way had been the only way. And she had done so well, she had no regrets. She adored her son and she loved her life in the theater.

Except now. Brant was back. She had been fine as long as he was living in the Hollywood dream world. But he wasn't an elusive memory. He was flesh and blood, and in Sarasota, Florida. Every day for the next three months he would be talking to her, touching her.

And she would want him again, but in three years she had grown too old to play with fire. She could tell by his eyes last night that he no longer considered her a child. She had also grown old enough to be fair game. Lord, she moaned silently. How was she going to cope? She couldn't run around acting like a spoiled, spiteful child. But she had to keep a distance.

Annoyed with her fear and confusion, Vickie jumped out of bed and into the shower. It was early, she thought wryly, but at least she wouldn't spend the morning rushing! By the time she finished scrubbing her skin, she felt she had the answers.

Polite and aloof. She could manage that. Again, her way would be the only way, especially when she still had feelings for him. Oh, not the puppy love of three years ago. But he was still and always would be her knight in shining armor no matter how mature or how capable she was, or how wonderful the life she had chosen was.

Block out the past, she told herself firmly, be polite and aloof. The summer could go smoothly. Besides, she was assuming a lot in imagining Brant was interested in her now. Terry was available, and the city was alive with attractive young women.

Yet her mind would not turn off as she dropped Mark at his school and finally parked at the theater. Pausing to brace herself mentally for the morning to come, she unconsciously checked her reflection in the rearview mirror. Had she changed much physically? Three years was not actually that great a span of time. Did one change externally as a result of internal changes?

To an extent. Her face had narrowed, increasing the height of her cheekbones and giving her a look of greater sophistication. The raven hair, which she had worn fairly short before, now waved down her spine. Monte liked her with long hair; it was useful for many of her roles, easily hidden when not.

Her nose hadn't changed any, but its imperious little tilt had its uses. It could give her the image of cool regality, an image she planned to rely on now.

The dining room, lit by the full glare of the houselights, was abuzz with conversation as she entered. Two tables were drawn together and the cast were sitting around them, sipping coffee, munching on danishes, and chatting. Vickie picked out Brant's blond head quickly and with dismay. The seat beside him was empty, obviously left for her. Monte would be to her right.

Squaring her shoulders, she sidled through the other tables and made her way to the group, chirping a pleasant "Good morning" that extended to everyone. The group answered her in a ragged chorus before returning to their individual conversations, except for Brant, and although he was being included in other discussions, his eyes were on her.

"Good morning, Miss Langley," he said gravely. His long arms, crooked at the elbow, were cast carelessly over the back of his chair. One jean-clad leg was crossed over the other casually. Part of his charisma, Vickie thought bitterly. No matter how far Brant went in his career, he could give the appearance of fitting in naturally anywhere.

"Good morning," she replied briefly, opening her script.

"We missed you last night," he continued, oblivious to her rebuff.

"Sorry." She hadn't meant to be curt. Her eyes rose unwittingly to his; something in his tone had compelled her to look at him. What she found in his intense cobalt gaze gave her shivers.

Time was playing tricks; fate was lending a hand. Brant Wicker was interested in her. He was more than interested; he was openly curious about her. He was evidently out to charm her. His look—warm but faintly grim and decidedly determined— told her simply that he meant to succeed.

"Okay," Monte announced, making his appearance from the stage in a brisk manner. "Cut the chatter. Work time. Vickie, did you have coffee yet? Get some." He stopped speaking for a moment as he took his chair to confer privately with Jim Ellery.

Brant was chuckling. "May I get your coffee for you, Miss Langley? I've heard you're never quite all here without it."

Vickie looked at him balefully, grinding her teeth. Apparently he had been discussing her with Monte, or the others, or both. She was famous for needing a cup of coffee to be completely lucid. He had been asking questions, and she didn't want any of his courteous concern.

"Thanks," she said stiffly. "I can get my own." Despite her resolve to be polite, her words carried the bite of rudeness. She winced; Bobby had heard her down at his end of the table and he was frowning, puzzled by her manner. She had to be careful.

"No need," Brant was replying pleasantly. "I'll get it. Black, right?" There was just a slight edge of sandpaper to his voice, implying that he realized she was purposely snubbing him.

"Right, thank you," she murmured, lowering her eyes to her script.

She thanked him again as he handed her a cup, avoiding his probing eyes. It was going to be harder than she thought to forget the past. It was going to be almost impossible with him sitting beside her. Three years might have never been. She could still remember the touch of the hands so close to hers, the heated strength of his thigh just inches away.

Nevertheless, the reading went well. The entire cast was in-

46

spired by the presence of the leading man, even Vickie. As straightforward as this simple read-through was, Brant's clear, low voice rang through the room with a sincere grasp of each and every of Shakespeare's often misunderstood innuendos. The entire room was so still when Harry Blackwell, reading Lodovico, came to the final line, that the proverbial pin could have been heard dropping.

"Good!" Monte declared, the first to speak. He scribbled on his script for several seconds before adding, "We'll finish here for the day. Tomorrow, a rough blocking of act one. If you're not in the act, you don't have to show."

Vickie, surprised that they had again been given extra hours of freedom, stayed seated for a minute, as they all did. Her hesitation proved to be her downfall.

"Well, Miss Langley," Brant drawled, twisting to her with a sardonic smile. "You can't have any emergency to rush off to now. Have some lunch with me."

"I can't—" Vickie began.

"Sure you can!" Monte interrupted, looking up from what Vickie had thought was intense concentration on his notes. What was he doing, feeding her to the lions with plate, napkin, and fork? "You don't have to pick up Mark for two hours!"

Vickie's cheeks burned. "I know," she protested quickly. "But I do have half a million other things to do and—"

"You couldn't possibly have been planning on doing them, because you didn't know we'd be breaking early!" Monte said firmly. "Go on with Brant, Vick. Entertain our guest and take it a little easy yourself!"

There was no polite excuse. She couldn't protest any further without appearing churlish. "A short lunch," she agreed, trying to appear indifferent rather than rude. "I really do have things that definitely do need doing." She managed an apologetic smile.

"A short lunch it will be," Brant promised, grinning devilishly as he waved a friendly good-bye to the others and proprietarily escorted her from the room. When they walked out into the sunlight, he indicated a shiny blue Mercedes, propelled her to it, and unerringly opened the passenger door and ushered her in with his customary gallantry. She settled warily into the plush interior.

"Where to?" he asked as he folded his own length into the car and turned to her, his powerful hands resting lightly on the steering wheel, his cobalt gaze unfathomable.

She lifted her shoulders in a shrug. "It doesn't matter."

Brant switched on the ignition. "All right, Miss Langley, I'll choose." He deftly manuevered the car from the parking lot and headed out on the highway. "If I remember correctly, and sometimes I do have a good memory, there's a nice little steak and seafood place not far from here. A hole in the wall, but clean, and the food is terrific."

Vickie turned her head to look out on the familiar scenery, convinced she was going to have to be as cold as possible. Brant seemed to be unaware that he was sitting next to an ice cube; he spoke occasionally as they drove, commenting on the growth of the city since he had last been here. Maintaining her vigil out the window, Vickie refrained from responding to his one-sided conversation, uttering a polite yes or no only when directly questioned. Hopefully he would eventually believe she found him boring, and even a composed ego couldn't tolerate such an insult!

The restaurant he brought her to was one she had never been to before, and not exactly a hole in the wall. It was on the beach, an atmospheric, thatched-roof, dark and cleverly decorated spot. Although expensive, as she realized on perusal of the menu, the dining room was comfortable and casual, intimate with a friendly warmth. Brant ordered a bottle of vintage wine before Vickie could stop him, and he overrode her order for a simple shrimp cocktail, insisting she try the Alaskan king crab legs, the house specialty.

His polite, faultless conversation continued until the wine arrived and the waitress went off to her other duties. Then he leaned forward, his eyes a hard, dark glitter in the glow of the single candle upon the table, and asked, "Okay, Miss Langley" —his voice was edged with derision—"would you mind telling me just what the problem is?"

His attack took her totally unawares and she stared at him

blankly, her fingers slowly tightening around the stem of her crystal wineglass. "Problem?" she echoed, annoyed to hear a quiver in her voice. Taking a deep breath, she steadied her tone. "I don't have any problem, Mr. Wicker, and if I did—not meaning to be rude—I doubt if I would feel inclined to discuss it with you."

"There is a problem. You do have a problem," he said grimly. "I assure you, it will only get worse if we don't come to an understanding." He leaned back in his chair and took a sip of his wine while studying her frozen face with an astute intensity.

She returned his scrutiny, her unwilling eyes drawn to his as if they were magnetized. If she had thought that there would be any Hollywood pretty-boy laxity to Brant, she had been sadly mistaken. He was the same man he had been, but three rough years older. Time had taken them both through worlds of rough lessons; if anything, he had matured now to a frightening, dominant virility that had nothing to do with his "star" status. The eyes that stared into hers were unmasked—dark, forceful, and determined with unconcealed annoyance, impatience, and anger.

"Well?" he prodded her with a deceiving softness.

"Brant," Vickie said with a sigh, folding her hands before her and watching her own fingers. "I know you are accustomed to having people fawning all over you. They like you sight unseen. This may strike you as inconceivable, and I'm sorry to be so blunt, but I personally don't care for you. Still, I don't see where that presents a tremendous problem. We have to work together, yes, but in our business we often have to work closely with people we don't particularly care for. We are both professionals. There will be no problems as far as the theater is concerned." Her speech was softly spoken, but arrogantly adamant. Not daring to face him, she kept her eyes on her own hands and waited for an explosion. She knew his cobalt stare was still relentlessly on her, she could sense it beyond a doubt, just as she could sense his very presence, his scent, his nearness. She knew his facial expression hadn't altered a hair.

"I don't believe you," he said calmly.

49

So much for the expected explosion. Vickie glanced back up at his words, astounded. They had been stated as simple fact.

"What don't you believe?" she asked, perplexed and irritated. He should have been angry, really angry, ready to wash his hands of her completely. "I assure you, Brant, that we can work together."

"*That* I don't doubt for an instant," he replied, cutting off his own speech as their food arrived and he thanked the young waitress, who recognized him with jittery awe and had difficulty keeping her mouth closed. After she had again disappeared into the kitchen, probably to tell the rest of the staff that *the* Brant Wicker was sitting in her station, he leaned forward once more and this time gripped Vickie's chin firmly so that she couldn't lower her eyes. "I don't believe that you don't like me."

"Of all the insufferable conceit!" Vickie blared out.

"Not conceit," he denied calmly, releasing his hold on her chin to pick up his cocktail fork and dig into the crab. "I believe there are lots of people in the world who may not particularly care for me. They may blatantly dislike me. What I don't believe is that you're one of them."

Vickie's own fork froze in the air with a morsel of tender white crab dangling from it as she stared at him, speechless. What was the matter with the man? She had been rude and blunt enough to lend credence to her words. "I—I suggest you start believing!" she said curtly, as unnerved as she had ever been three years ago. "It's true!" Except the statement rang false and hollow to her own ears.

He smiled unexpectantly, easing the grimness of his angular features. "It isn't true. I told you, I do have a good memory sometimes, and, Vickie, I remember we were more than friends. We didn't part as enemies. So what I don't understand is why we can't be friends now."

"What difference does it make?" she flashed irritably.

"A lot, to me."

"Why?" Vickie demanded with exasperation, toying with her food.

"Because," he said softly, "I remember all that you can be. A

Victoria as honest and open as the morning sun. A woman full of feeling, vibrancy, and compassion." As he spoke, his hand moved across the table to cover hers and envelop it in warmth and a gentle, rugged strength.

Flushing, Vickie pulled her hand away. He didn't stop her. She took a long swallow of her wine before remembering that white wine had precipitated her downfall with him once before. Setting the glass down firmly, she quietly began. "Mr. Wicker—"

"What is this Mr. Wicker bit?" he interrupted irritably. His eyes glittered into hers with an edge of mockery as he dropped civility for insinuation. "Don't you think such formality is a little ridiculous?"

"No, I don't," she replied coolly.

"You know my name; I've heard you use it nicely."

"All right, *Brant,*" Vickie hissed, challenging him with stormy gray eyes. "You're talking about three years ago. A night that didn't mean a damn thing to either of us. Now you've sailed back in here, and I should be willing to pick up where you left off, except there's nothing to be picked up. If you're looking for a few hot dates while in town now, try Terry."

"Good Lord, woman!" he ejaculated angrily. "I am not looking for a few hot dates. I've had enough so-called 'hot dates' to last ten lifetimes. I'm not looking for anything. I want to know why you're avoiding me and what the hell I could have done to you."

"You didn't do anything to me," Vickie stated tonelessly, actually meaning what she said. He hadn't done anything to her; she had done it all to herself. But he had been the unwitting accomplice in the greatest humiliation and trauma of her life. That she couldn't explain. "Brant, I'm just not a starry-eyed kid anymore. I don't want to be your summer entertainment. To be blunt, I simply have no desire to jump back in bed with you."

"I don't recall asking you to," he said with an arched brow.

"Then why don't you just leave me alone?" she wailed, frustrated and annoyed by his sardonic response.

"I have no intention of leaving you alone," he grinned, show-

51

ing a mouthful of perfect white teeth before biting calmly into a clump of butter-drenched crab. He chewed and swallowed, watching her speculatively before adding, "I've thought of you frequently during the last three years. And I think I know you better than you give me credit for. I'm going to hound you mercilessly until I discover just why you're behaving like a spoiled brat toward me."

"That's a discovery you'll never make!" Vickie lashed out in cold defense, realizing with horror what she had said only after the incriminating words were out of her mouth.

"Ah-hah!" Brant exclaimed, delving back into his crab. "The truth leaks out!"

"Will you stop," Vickie grumbled. "There is no truth." She feigned a great interest in the rim of her wineglass. Damn! She couldn't allow herself to fall into his goading, persistent traps. "There is no truth," she repeated. "My life is hectic, that's all. I don't have time to run around worrying about you."

"I see. You don't have time to be civil."

"Okay, Brant," Vickie acknowledged. "I haven't been particularly civil. Haven't you heard of people having bad days?"

"Sure, but that isn't the case now, is it?" He took her hand again before she could withdraw it, sending a tingling sensation through her arm, which ended as a trembling shiver throughout her body. Feeling the shiver, he grinned. "Listen, Victoria," he said in that soft voice of his that served only to underline grim determination. "I'm not an idiot. I know something is wrong. I've seen you pretty cool, but this is different. Waspish arrogance is not you. But I'll make a deal with you. I won't pry—for the time being at least—if you'll make an attempt to act like Vickie around me."

"Brant!" she declared, trying to break the magnetic spell of his eyes. "I'm not Mary Poppins!"

"I know that!" he laughed, a finger tracing the outer edges of the hand he held.

"I don't want to be your lover!" she snapped.

"Only time will tell the truth to that," he mused, nonplussed.

"Please . . ." Vickie grated out, irritated that his touch seemed

Don't keep trying to tell me it was nothing to you. Your sheet trick was clever, but I wasn't all that drunk. You were a virgin that night—"

"Brant!" Vickie fought the flush that rose to her cheeks. "I don't even remember!"

"The hell you don't!" he growled forcefully, and the hard set to his well-defined chin kept her from protesting afresh.

She glanced uneasily around before leaning toward him, the hardness in her stare equaling his. "I repeat," she stated heatedly. "What difference does any of this make now? You keep talking about three irrelevant years ago! I've been married since. I've had a child. You've had your numerous affairs. We are working together now, and that's all. I don't like to discuss the past!"

"I'm discussing the past so that we can get to the future," Brant said, strumming forceful fingers upon the table. "Methinks, my lady, that thou doth protest too much," he quoted lightly. "And I also think you're one hell of a liar."

"Brant—"

"No, *Vickie.*" He cut her off firmly, his eyes blazing despite his low tone. "I came back here for Monte, but I came back for another reason too. You, my dear Miss Langley. In all my consequent 'affairs' as you call them, I've been looking for something. Something real, something honest. Something we could have had."

"Don't!" Vickie objected fiercely. "Talk about liars! You walked out of here with nothing on your mind but your star-studded future! You're inventing things that didn't exist! You're all talk, and I'm just too old to fall for it."

"Wrong!"

The ogling waitress brought the credit card and form to the table and Brant and Vickie both fell silent as he signed in a large distinct flourish. Preoccupied, Brant still gave the girl a polite smile, obligingly signing the autographs she requested with a pleasant banter. Lulled by his tone, Vickie began to believe their too personal conversation would be over.

But when the waitress had gone, he turned back to her with

none of his grim fervor lost. "Wrong, Vickie. I'm not talk—you know damned well I never was."

"You're a Hollywood star," she sniffed derisively.

"I'm a man," he corrected her quietly. "The same man I was before. I happen to be an actor, which makes it rather incongruous that an actress should scorn my livelihood."

Vickie inclined her head skeptically. "Sorry."

Rising, Brant assisted her from her chair. She was forced into greater awareness of his dominating physique. An involuntary shiver rippled down her spine, and she felt her breathing grow ragged.

"Come, my lady," he chuckled, his voice deep and throaty in her ear, "and I'll shortly relieve you of my proximity."

She graced him with a very baleful glare that caused his grin to deepen devilishly. "I'll relieve you of my proximity for the time, that is," he promised with amused solemnity. "You are going to be seeing a lot of me."

"Really? Your confidence is amazing."

He shrugged. "Maybe. But I wouldn't suggest a wager against me. I want you, my sweet leading lady, and I intend to get you."

The door to the restaurant swung shut behind them and Vickie turned to him bitterly as they strolled for the Mercedes.

"I thought you weren't going to ask me to bed."

"I haven't—yet. We're going to start with basics."

"You'll excuse me," she retorted, raising an arched brow as he ushered her into the passenger seat, "if I don't happen to be around for your basics, since I've stated I'm not interested in the finale."

His annoying, knowing grin never left his face. His blue eyes raked over her form in a probing, assessing gaze.

"You'll be around. We both know it. The only one you're lying to is yourself. Why, I don't know. But I think I've already solved half of my dilemma. You're afraid of me. Now, the question is why."

CHAPTER THREE

"Scene three—five minutes."

Jim was a damned good stage manager, Vickie mused idly as she watched him call his command. A no-nonsense person, he seldom smiled or joined in any of the revelry natural to the cast. But he held their respect. He kept the troop together and had a talent for whipping them into shape when necessary. Monte, although a superb director, was too much of a nice guy. He was personally attached to each of his cast members. At times he'd yell, but then would become pliable in their hands.

Chewing on the nub of her pencil, her legs stretched comfortably on the chair before her, Vickie decided the two men were a great pair. Monte was genius; Jim was discipline.

Brant, she admitted grudgingly, was both in one. When he rehearsed, he was business. He didn't miss a cue, he didn't cause a minute's waste of time. He accepted direction gracefully while still imbuing his character with the irrefutable uniqueness of his talent. Offstage, he would tease. He had already brought the entire cast and crew around to lighthearted acceptance. He was the star, the big man brought in for the season. But no one would ever know it. Which was nice, Vickie thought dryly. His down-to-earth humanity had been one of the things she had once loved him for. . . .

Except now, she was heartily resenting him. It would have been a hell of a lot easier to deal with an egotistical snob whom everyone else was having difficulty stomaching. She was the only one feigning polite welcome. But then she was the only one wishing Brant back in his Beverly Hills manor or Madison Avenue town house.

And she was the only one who knew he was capable of being ruthlessly demanding and persistent. It was doubtful that anyone could underestimate him. Perpetually polite and especially pleasant to those who were nervous around him, Brant wore a tangible aura of determination. If his height and lean, muscled build did not quell a stout heart, the strong line of his profile and piercing intensity of his eyes would. With a quirk of amusement Vickie decided he was not a person she would like to run into in a dark alley at night.

Monte, sitting beside her, stretched, groaned, and rubbed the back of his neck before casting a glance her way. "How was lunch?"

The question startled her. She had been sitting next to him for the past two hours, watching the progression of the first two scenes—scenes in which Desdemona didn't appear. He had spoken to her only occasionally, and then only to make a general comment or issue a rhetorical question that he would immediately answer himself.

"Lunch was fine," she told him, assuming a casual tone even as she attempted too late to hide a frown. She could still remember and bristle at the memory of Brant laughing at her when she haughtily informed him she was definitely not afraid of him.

"What have you got against Brant?" Monte quizzed her pointedly.

"Nothing!" Vickie protested. She shifted her legs and crossed one ankle over the other, comfortable in her jeans.

"You're bristling!" Monte chuckled. "I don't believe it, and I love it. My little, untouchable Ice Maiden bristling!"

"I am not bristling," Vickie objected with a sigh. "I'm just not all that enamored of the man. And I'm not really sure why you brought him in for *Othello*. The dark man? The moor?" She laughed, pointing her pencil at Brant who was still onstage conversing with Bobby, who was playing Iago. "You couldn't have found a man more fair if you would have scoured half the country."

58

Monte gave her his full, reproachful attention. "You've heard him," he told her sternly. "His Shakespeare is untouchable. I've seen him do this particular play before with remarkable results. You know yourself what can be done with good stage makeup." Shrugging, Monte continued with even a stronger note of rebuke. "Brant is an exceptional actor. He could walk on that stage in jeans and a T-shirt and by the time he walked off half the audience would be ready to swear he had been in period costume."

"I suppose you're right," Vickie said noncommittally.

"Damn right, I'm right!" Monte agreed. "And as a favor to me, I'd like you to act a little more decently. I was lucky to get him. He only came here as a personal favor. You know I couldn't possibly pay the salary he could be receiving elsewhere."

"Well," Vickie said curtly, "he should have come as a personal favor to you. There wouldn't have been a Brant Wicker if it weren't for you."

Monte waved a thin hand in the air dismissively. "That's where you're wrong, Vick, and I think you know it. Brant would have gotten a break somewhere else. He never needed much luck; he had talent."

Vickie said nothing in reply. She was being churlish, and she knew it. She couldn't deny Brant's acting ability, and she winced at herself as she argued against him. Had they never met, she would have been thrilled with the prospect of sharing the stage with him. She deplored her own attitude and made a mental note to keep her personal feelings entirely to herself. It was sad to pride oneself on professional ethics and sophisticated work habits and then turn around and sound like a spiteful ingenue.

"Onstage. Scene three!" Jim called.

"You heard my main man," Monte said, smiling at her wryly. There were times when Jim even told Monte what to do.

"Yes, and I'm rushing to obey!" Vickie chuckled. Springing to her feet with script and pencil in hand, she started for the stage.

"Victoria." Monte stopped her quietly.

She stopped at once and glanced back at him curiously.

"I meant what I said. Please be decent to Brant." Seeing the stubborn set to her chin, he added softly, "Please. I'm not threatening you, you know that. Just be nice and decent for me."

"Monte!" Vickie chuckled, a mischievous twinkle flickering in her eyes. "When am I ever indecent?" Sobering, she added, "I'm sorry, Monte. You're right, Brant is exceptional; we're lucky to have him. And I shall be charming and entirely decent!"

She spun gracefully around and bound for the stage, accepting a hand from Bobby to leap up to the planking.

Monte's voice took on its professional "directorial" tone. "Duke, senators, upstage right at the table. Messenger, Brabantio, Othello, Iago, Roderigo, and Desdemona, offstage left. Go!"

Blocking was slow and tedious. It was a time when the actors were free to speak, make suggestions, voice complaints, and clarify misunderstandings of any lines. Vickie, who didn't enter until halfway through the scene, when she was called upon to declare her love for her new husband before her father and the duke, sat on the planked floor for thirty minutes before she heard her own cue, the final line of a speech by her father.

Her part of the scene went well. Only moments later, the duke, the senator, and others made their exits. Then came Othello's final line entreating her to come with him: "Come Desdemona, I have but an hour of love, of worldly matters and direction, to spend with thee. We must obey the time."

"Put your arm around her waist," Monte directed Brant. "Vickie, you do the same, but slowly as you watch him, having the action last while you walk offstage."

Brant did not move his arm as they reached the wing. "You can let go now," Vickie said dryly.

He complied with a grin. "Pity. Although who knows? By the time we reach act five, I may be happy to smother you."

"I guess I'm lucky this is just a play," she replied sweetly. Damn! So much for decency, but there was something about his look and touch that goaded her, no matter how earnest her intentions were to be pleasant.

"I guess you are," Brant smiled, his voice subdued, belying his

60

true thoughts. His blue gaze swept her briefly. "Excuse me, I promised to watch the end of the scene for Bobby."

He turned on his heels and left her with the silent agility of a cat to take a seat near Monte and focus on the speeches of Iago and Roderigo that ended the act. Vickie remained behind the drawn curtain and sank weakly to the floor, furious to find herself shaking. She couldn't go on like this, being affected by every encounter with him. They were acting, but his possessive hand on her hip had sent shivers racing down her spine. But he had walked away from her. That was what she wanted. He had said he intended to have her, yet today he was almost ignoring her.

Good. She was beginning to feel an irresistible tug to respond, to savor his touch whenever it fell her way. Oh, no! she wailed silently to herself. Not again. Never again. No matter what he said about his feelings, about being "a little bit in love," she knew him! His love was an expansive thing. He was going to leave again, as he had before. And he would be "a little bit in love" a dozen times.

No. She would never set herself up for another fall. It was a good thing, a marvelous thing, that he had dropped all pretense and chosen to ignore her.

They ran the full act once more, surprisingly smoothly, before Monte told them all they could leave after he had given them each a few personal notes and instructions. Quickly heading for the door, Vickie was stopped by Brant's all-encompassing call. "Hey! Has anybody seen my script?"

Sighing, Vickie stopped walking and returned to the tables where they had scattered their belongings. They were an ensemble; if one member had a problem, all helped to solve it so Connie, Bobby, and Terry were crawling around the tables.

"How about backstage?" Vickie asked Brant.

He shrugged. "Good idea. Thanks."

She nervously followed him back to the left wing, where he did find the script on the podium. "Found it!" His voice rang out. "Thanks, everyone!"

"Well, see you tomorrow," Vickie murmured politely, remembering her resolution.

"I'll see you tonight," he corrected her.

Startled, she glanced at him warily, wondering what he now intended to contrive. But he wore that expression of amusement that never failed to irritate her. He knew her thoughts.

"Prickly, aren't you?" he drawled, his stillness denoting a leashed energy that was all the more potent and vital. "I come at night," he told her, chuckling, "to help Smoky in the scene shop. Not to attack unwilling actresses."

"I hardly thought you intended to attack me," Vickie replied airily. "Good-bye."

She knew he watched her as she walked away, and she knew he still grinned with that knowing amusement. The hell with him, she decided.

Chin held high, she walked briskly through the empty dining room out to the Volvo, supremely agitated and thoroughly furious with herself for being upset in the first place. What the hell was happening to her? Brant was just a man, and she knew how to deal with men.

Still, she practically ripped the car door from its hinges. Gritting her teeth, she decided it was better to take her frustrations out on the steel of the car than to expose them as she had with Monte. Sticking her key into the ignition with a vengeance, she was further irritated to find the old Volvo refusing to start. And in her reckless irritation she quickly flooded the engine.

Unbelieving, she kept at the car, knowing she should leave it alone, but unable to do so. Finally she pulled the key from the starter with disgust. She crawled out of the car, and sure she was alone, kicked a wheel viciously.

Chastising herself as she admitted defeat, she looked around the parking lot hastily for a ride. Bobby's white Cutlass was just pulling out to the highway and she raced after it, slowing when she realized he was too far away and would never see her. Even as she waved her arms frantically, the Cutlass became swallowed up in the afternoon traffic. Disgusted, Vickie walked back to the

Volvo, bitterly wondering why her day was going so badly. Everyone was gone.

Except Brant. He was leaning against the Volvo, his frame imposing against the compact car, his arms casually crossed as a subtle half grin lit his face. His golden hair rippled in the slight breeze, that one unruly piece softly draped over his forehead. "Having a problem?" he inquired.

"Obviously," she retorted.

"Kicking the car does nothing for the engine," he commented.

"Really?" It was a pity she couldn't kick him. "If you'll excuse me, I'll just try the engine again."

"That's foolish. Your starter just isn't flicking over."

Vickie delicately arched a cynical brow. "I didn't realize you were a mechanic as well as a star. If you don't mind, I'll just try it once more."

Brant shrugged and leisurely stepped aside. "See you later." He walked to his own Mercedes as Vickie slipped back into her car.

He was, of course, right. The car simply wasn't turning over, and she knew she merely flooded the engine worse with every attempt.

It was getting later and later and Mark would be waiting. Wincing, Vickie looked through her rearview mirror to see Brant in the driver's seat of his car. His engine was spinning to life and he was about to drive away. Which is exactly what she deserved. She had hardly been gracious.

In consternation she chewed on her lip. The thought of having Brant see Mark was appalling, but the nursery would be closing shortly. She had to pick up Mark, and Brant was the only transportation available. It was inevitable that he would see the child sometime during the summer. She might as well start her string of lies now, that is if she could still catch him. The Mercedes was pulling from its parking space as she realized desperately that she really had no choice. But damn, it was going to be galling to ask for a ride.

Slamming out of the Volvo, she wondered if Brant would drive past her after her rudeness. But he didn't, of course, and she experienced a moment of shame over her own cattiness. At twenty-five, she should be able to accept his teasing banter as easily as she accepted Bobby's good-natured innuendos. She should be able to smile and shrug as she had with any other man.

But Brant wasn't any other man. He was made of relentless, persistent steel. And he was the one man in the world that no amount of logic could keep her from wanting and still loving.

He didn't make her come to him; he stopped the Mercedes next to her. "Can I give you a ride?"

"Yes, thank you."

He pushed open the passenger door. "Enter, the chariot awaits." His eyes were on the road as she slid beside him. "I believe we have to pick up a child?"

"Yes, if you don't mind," Vickie replied, somewhat surprised that he would remember such a thing. She gave him the address of the nursery school.

"I have a feeling," Brant commented dryly, "that your son is the only reason you're in this car with me. If it were only you," he chuckled, "I believe you might walk ten miles out of spite."

"I'm not spiteful," Vickie said quietly.

"No?" he queried pleasantly, "Not the type to cut off your nose to pay back your face, huh?"

"I rather hope not," Vickie murmured, surprised by his almost playful tone. She glanced at him uneasily, but he seemed to have nothing beyond driving on his mind. "The school is right around the corner," she advised him as they neared the end of the block. "Just pull into the driveway by the gate; his teacher will bring him out."

Trying not to stare directly at Brant, Vickie was tense and compelled to watch him as Mark appeared. Did she detect a faint narrowing of his eyes? Or was it merely her own guilt? Surely not guilt. She had nothing to be guilty about. Brant had never known about Mark; all that was between them was an accident of biology.

"He's a beautiful child," was Brant's only reference to the boy as Mark toddled to the car on his stubby legs, then stopped abruptly as he saw the stranger.

"Come on, sweetheart," Vickie urged her child, opening the door to scoop him up beside her. "This, Mark, is Mr. Wicker—"

"Hey! Don't teach him that!" Brant protested. "Mark, my name is Brant." He made no effort to touch the little boy, but grinned at him invitingly.

Mark continued to eye him warily, his bright little gaze popping to his mother and then back to Brant. "Brant," he repeated, saying the name with surprising accuracy.

"That's right. Brant. Mr. Wicker is quite a mouthful, and quite unnecessary."

The car pulled back out on the street before Brant turned back to Vickie. "Where to now?"

"Oh!" Vickie had been so involved in watching Brant's reaction to Mark that she had forgotten he didn't know where she lived. Mumbling her address, she buried her face in her son's black curls.

"How old is he?" Brant asked, and Vickie covertly watched for any sign of suspicion in his features. There was none, none that was discernible. It was a perfectly normal question to ask about a child. She was growing paranoid. No, she wasn't growing paranoid. She had been paranoid since Brant had appeared.

"Not quite two," Vickie replied, calculating quickly in her head.

"He's a big boy."

"Yes, uh, his father was a large man." Eager to change the subject, Vickie rushed on apologetically. "I'm sorry to have you driving around like this. I know you must have other things to do—"

"No, not a thing in the world!" Brant interrupted. "I don't mind picking Mark up at all. I like kids."

Vickie pulled her head up from Mark's and openly stared at Brant. He hadn't made his statement off-handedly as so many people did to be polite. He meant it. He sincerely liked children. And he must have spent time around them, because he hadn't come on too strong at the first introduction to Mark. He sensed that children needed to come to adults in their own time.

"Brant."

"Hmm?"

"I—" She what? She knew she owed him an apology. "I'm sorry I was so rude. I really needed this ride, and I'm grateful you waited."

"Think nothing of it," he returned easily, allowing his eyes to wander from the road to hers for a mischievous look. "Actually I'm finagling for a dinner invitation."

His open good-humor was impossible to resist. Vickie laughed, more at ease now that Brant had seen Mark, and, as she had previously assured herself without conviction, had not noticed a thing unusual about the child.

"All right," she told him with a hint of amusement. "You've got yourself a dinner invitation. Except you're going to have to take pot luck."

"I'm crazy about pot luck," he assured her gravely. "Is this it?"

They had pulled in front of the modest, old, Spanish-style home that Vickie had purchased after taking the job at Monte's. She was grateful that she had recently mown the lawn and trimmed the profusion of hibiscus and crotons that rimmed the house and the neatly tiled walk.

"This is it."

Mark, glad to be home, bounded to the ground and scampered up the walk as Vickie more sedately got out of the car, fumbling for her keys in her bag.

"Allow me," Brant said, taking the keys from her fingers to dexterously open the front door. He paused as he followed Vickie in, his gaze sweeping over the room. Once again she was grateful she had a habit of straightening up before she left the house in the morning.

"This is nice," Brant said, assessing the room as he closed the door behind him and went over to sit nonchalantly on the cranberry-cushioned white wicker divan, his fingers locked behind his head.

"Thanks," Vickie replied, moving into the living room to cast her script and bag down on the oak coffee table. Now that she had him in her house, she felt strangely tongue-tied. Even Mark

66

had deserted her, having ambled into his own room. "Can I get you anything, Brant?"

"Not a thing." He grinned satyrlike and patted the divan. "Sit down."

His words gave her an alarming sense of déjà-vu, but she agreeably complied, sitting at an angle so that she faced him without being too close.

"So," he murmured, his blue gaze casually moving from the decor of the house to sweep over Vickie, "tell me about Victoria Langley."

She shrugged and vaguely lifted a hand. "The story isn't very thrilling. I landed a job in Charleston, then wound up back here at Monte's. That's it. The Brant Wicker story has to be a lot more interesting."

He raised both brows and emitted a long stream of breath. "Actually, the Brant Wicker story is incredibly boring. I spent two years doing that inane sit-com, then I did that inane space movie. Then a show on Broadway, which I did enjoy doing. Not that I'm not grateful to the 'inane' TV series or the 'inane' movie. Between the two of them, I became financially independent. I can choose now to do whatever I want, and my next project should be a good one."

"Oh?" Vickie couldn't help but ask. "What is your next project?"

"A movie, but a good one this time. A remake of an old Hitchcock thriller."

"That's good," Vickie murmured. "I'm happy for you."

"You really are, aren't you?" he mused, reaching to touch her chin.

"Of course, why not?" she replied, flushing and catching his hand.

The grip she held subtly switched so that he was holding her, fascinated as he drew idle patterns on her veins. "I guess I'll always remember Lenore."

"Ah, but you loved Lenore!" Vickie reminded him.

He chuckled with no bitterness. "I don't think Lenore or I ever had a great love for each other. We were both just there."

Like I'm "just here" now! Vickie warned herself, willing the exciting sensation of his light touch upon her hand to go away. But futilely.

"Have you heard from Lenore recently?" she asked with indifference.

"Not from her, but of her," he replied honestly. He glanced at Vickie and his grin broadened. "She married a used-car salesman in Pittsburgh. I hear he doesn't allow her out of the house. Smart fellow."

Again Vickie couldn't help but laugh. It was a fitting end for the conniving Lenore.

"Now," Brant started to say as Vickie suddenly realized that he was holding her hand so that she couldn't possibly escape him, "let's get back to Victoria Langley. And back to Mr. Langley. Do you still miss him?"

"I—ummm." Vickie's gray eyes fell like a lead balloon. She might be an actress, but as an out-and-out liar she was poor. It had been so long since she had had to invent a story. Her private life was considered private at Monte's; the only one who ever pried was Terry, and avoiding Terry was merely a nuisance.

Trying to lie to Brant was another matter. For one thing, his questions terrified her, constricting her throat. She had too much at stake. For another, he was so above board himself. She couldn't imagine him lying for any reason. And she had the uncanny suspicion that his piercing eyes could detect a falsehood before it was ever uttered.

"No," she said, not trying to disengage her hand. "But, er, Mark's father is a subject I'd rather not discuss."

"Then we won't discuss him," Brant said softly.

Mark himself chose that moment to come toddling back into the room with his collection of small *Star Wars* toys. From the corner of her eye Vickie could see that Brant's features had twisted into a puzzled frown.

"I had blond curls like his black ones," he said idly. Catching Vickie watching him, he added sheepishly, "My mother still has them in a Baggie!"

Vickie laughed with him, but the sound seemed to be stran-

68

gling in her throat. It turned to a cough. "Langley was very dark," she heard herself saying. "His hair was darker than mine. And he . . . he had the curls until . . ."

She had expected Brant to bail her out, to apologize for bringing up a painful subject, but he didn't. His frown deepened. "Why do you keep referring to him as Langley?"

"Pardon?" Vickie blinked rapidly.

"Your husband. You call him Langley."

"It was his name," Vickie said blankly.

"Yes, I know," Brant persisted impatiently. "But most wives or widows refer to their spouses by their given names. What was Langley's given name?"

"Mark," Vickie said quickly. In a single movement she jerked her hand away and sprang to her feet, unable to sit still for the conversation any longer. "I'd better check the refrigerator if we're going to have dinner," she garbled in haste. "Just make yourself at home."

"I will," he promised.

"And—"

"And I'll keep an eye on Mark. In fact, if it's all right with you, I'll take him outside for a bit and let him play."

"Sure," Vickie murmured queasily, "if he'll go with you."

She was chagrined to see her two-year-old accept Brant's hand and invitation for "Outside?" without hesitation. And she had to bite her lip to keep from thinking her own son a traitor.

"Go on," she said with a helpless sigh. "Dinner will be about an hour."

She turned quickly for the swinging shuttered doors that led to the kitchen, not wanting to watch as the two heads, one tiny with raven curls, the other blond and high atop broad shoulders, as they exited by the front door. She was glad in a way that the afternoon had been forced upon her; it was a relief to no longer fear Brant's seeing her son and coming to an immediate conclusion. But she wondered if she would ever get over feeling uneasy.

Vickie was grateful to find that she had several strip steaks in the freezer. Despite their frozen state, they would broil quickly. Setting them on the counter to be forked and seasoned, she prepared a quick broccoli and cheese casserole and peeled potatoes to mash. She kept telling herself that Brant had cajoled her into inviting him for dinner, and if her culinary skills didn't please him, he'd be smart enough to dine elsewhere in the future. Nevertheless, she took great pains with the simple menu, dressing the table with a fine linen cloth, her English bone china, a spray of flowers, and two candles. She was nothing short of ingenious, she decided wryly as she surveyed her efforts before returning to the kitchen to throw the steaks under the broiler.

She didn't see Brant, nor hear him come in. The sensuous, masculine scent that usually warned her of his presence was blotted out by the aroma of the broiling meat. She didn't know he had entered until his arms slipped around her waist and he whispered into her ear, "That smells delicious!"

She must have jumped three feet, which caused him to laugh a hearty, irritating laugh. "I don't bite," he told her.

"I know," she replied acidly, without thinking. "You only nibble."

His arms were still locked around her waist, holding her tightly to him, her hips pressed against his. His brows arched high as she struggled to free herself from his grasp.

But he wasn't letting go. "My, Victoria," he said mockingly, "it seems that you too have a memory."

Vickie stopped struggling, to stare at him in open-mouthed dismay. Brant's eyes kindled their fire of piercing blue ice, then his lips descended to take full advantage of the situation. They lowered over Vickie's with a swift and firm persuasion that momentarily took her breath away. Too stunned to protest, she felt her mouth sweetly invaded by the probing warmth of his tongue, and her form crushed more tightly to his. His fingers splayed across the small of her back, making the contact between them so intimate that their clothing might not have existed. She could vibrantly feel his heat, and his lean corded muscles as her arms fell to his shoulders. There was a warning sounding in her head, but she seemed powerless to listen or obey. Brant didn't intend for the kiss to be quick or easily forgotten. His hands began a lulling massage down her back as his mouth continued

70

to plunder deeply—exploring, savoring, leaving her so breathless that she was pliant, too weak to object to his assault in any way.

It wasn't fair, she thought vaguely, he was stronger. But she was lying to herself if she believed strength alone kept her in his arms. His heady scent now overpowered that of the food, and the commanding magic of his hands upon her back was hypnotizing. She could remember the touch of his fingers upon her bare skin, remember with delight that his lips could weave exotic spells on any part of her flesh, and as clear as yesterday she could remember his magnificent body melded to hers, creating nothing short of ecstasy. An ecstasy that brought the agony of deprivation. Brant gave with every part of himself, except for his heart. . . .

Humiliated and horrified by the intensity of excitement that stirred so easily within her at his practiced conquest, Vickie finally found the strength to fight against him. And now he released her instantly, smiling with the satisfaction of the victor.

"Damn you!" Vickie cried hoarsely. "Don't you ever do that again. You have no right . . . I invited you to dinner—"

"I know," he grinned wickedly, undaunted by her clenched-fist fury. "You invited me to dinner, not to bed. But you don't see me dragging you anywhere."

She was tempted to slap his smug, handsome features. "I hardly think even you, Brant, would drag a woman off to bed with her two-year-old son sitting in the next room!" Enraged, she kept on, heedless of what she was saying. "Now you can understand why I don't care to see you! I don't feel like being the victim of another ra—"

She broke off her own word, appalled and sorry as she saw his lips go white in a thin tense line and his eyes harden to gems of deep indigo. His voice, when he uttered the single word, completing her sentence, was a deceptively calm whisper. "Rape?"

Flushing furiously, Vickie closed her eyes and spun away from him, rubbing her temple.

"I think we both know how ridiculous that was," he spat out contemptuously. "If that was a rape, it was surely the most provoked in history."

71

"The steaks!" Vickie shrieked, wishing against all odds that they could simply forget the interlude.

But that wasn't going to happen. Brant had reached the breaking point of his usually concealed, infamous temper. His arm clamped onto Vickie's and he spun her back around like a disc. "The hell with the steaks!" he thundered. "Is that what all this standoffishness has been about? This rude, touch-me-not behavior. You've deluded yourself into believing that you were *raped* by me?"

"No!" Vickie whispered miserably, her eyes upon his white-knuckled grip that was turning her arm the same pasty color. "No!" she repeated. "I didn't mean to say that. I was angry. I—please, let go of me."

Startled, he looked at his own hand. Muttering an oath, he released his grip to stride past her.

"What are you doing?" she cried, frightened by the violence of his movement.

"I'm getting your steaks out before they burn," he replied curtly, snatching a potholder from the wall to remove the sizzling meat. He set the broiler tray upon the waiting hot pad and tossed the potholder back down, stalking furiously for the swinging doors. Stopping abruptly, he swung back to her sharply on a single heel. "And now, Miss Langley, I'm checking on your son."

Not interested in any further comments she might have to make, he slammed against the door and went out, leaving it swinging erratically in his wake.

Mark, she thought sickly. She had momentarily forgotten about her son while Brant, thoroughly irate, had remembered him. Snapping herself from the trauma enveloping her, Vickie transferred the meat to a serving platter. She wondered if Brant still intended to stay for dinner, or if he was going to walk out as soon as she brought the food to the table. He should leave. It would be for the best. They should stay enemies for the entire summer. But despite herself she was hoping he wouldn't.

He was sitting on the divan, rolling a small ball back and forth to Mark, who sat delightedly a few feet away on the floor. Vickie silently began to set the various platters on the table. "Can I do anything?" Brant inquired coldly.

"No," Vickie murmured. "Ah, yes," she added. "You can pour the wine."

The silence between them was stiff and ominous as they finished setting the table together. Only Mark chattered on, pleased that his new friend seemed to be staying. Brant heaved him high into the air before situating him in his booster chair, the dark glower of his fair features receding as the little boy whooped with laughter.

"He's young to sit at such an elegant table so nicely," Brant commented as he pulled back Vickie's chair for her to sit.

He was young, Vickie thought proudly, ready to break the ice that Brant had begun to chisel. "He's an only child," she explained modestly. "He goes many places with me, and he's been dining out in restaurants since he was an infant." She didn't add that she had simply been lucky with Mark. He was innately fastidious; he ate neatly and kept his toys in order.

From Mark they went on to discuss the theater, Brant complimenting Monte's current production of *Godspell*, then moving on to talk about their upcoming work in *Othello*. Dinner passed swiftly and comfortably, with Brant insisting afterward that he help with the dishes. Vickie was keenly aware of him beside her as they performed their after-dinner domestic tasks together, but he made no further attempt to touch her, nor were any of his comments even remotely personal. It seemed they had reached a stalemate.

They had eaten dinner early, so there was plenty of time left for coffee. Vickie insisted Brant retreat into the living room while she prepared the coffee, telling him he had been more than a helpful guest.

"Damn!" she exclaimed suddenly as she brought the coffee out to the living room to join him. "I forgot about my car!"

"Don't worry about it," Brant told her, picking up his cup. "I'll take a look at it when we go back to the theater. Believe it or not," he told her wryly, "I am somewhat of a mechanic. And if I can't find the problem, I'll have it towed to a garage."

73

"Thanks," Vickie murmured, sipping her own coffee as she wondered what Brant's public would think. So far the big "star" had acted as chauffeur, entertained a toddler, washed dishes, and sat to dinner at an ordinary table. Now he was going to play grease monkey.

She was startled when the phone rang. Excusing herself, she was dismayed to find upon answering that the caller was Mrs. Gimball.

"Vickie, dear," the lady began with abject remorse, "I do hate to call you like this, but there's simply no help for it! I was so stupid! I just scalded my left hand pouring tea and I'm afraid I have to go to the hospital to have it treated. I hate to leave you in such a spot—"

"Mrs. Gimball!" Vickie protested vehemently, knowing full well her dependable sitter would never call to cancel unless it were a true emergency. "Don't you dare sit there apologizing to me! You go and get that taken care of right away!"

"I hope you can work something out." Mrs. Gimball fretted. "I'm so sorry—"

"Please, stop worrying," Vickie begged. "And get on to the hospital. That burn must be killing you right now. Can you drive? Shall I come and get you?" Vickie was aware she didn't have her own car, but she was certain Brant would not object to such a mission.

"No, no," Mrs. Gimball assured her quickly. "My son is coming to get me. You worry about yourself and that little boy."

Slowly replacing the receiver after hurried good-byes, Vickie sagged against the wall. What else could happen today? Nibbling at a long, bronze nail, she worried over what to do about Mark. Her parents would happily watch him, but they were in Bradenton. Her brother, Edward, would also cheerfully help her out, but he was an hour away in St. Petersburg. Sighing, she decided she would have to call Harry Blackwell's wife, Cathy. But that meant that Vickie would have to take Mark over there and leave him for the night.

"A problem?"

Brant was standing in the hallway, hands on hips, astute blue eyes gazing at her. She looked for a hint of mockery in his features, but there was none.

"Yes, a real problem," she answered him idly, thinking even as she spoke. "My baby-sitter has had an accident." She picked the receiver up while mentally conjuring a picture of the Blackwells' number. "Excuse me," she told Brant, remembering he stood before her, "I have to do something rather quickly."

Brant wedged the phone firmly from her fingers. Startled by his action, and annoyed by the electricity of his touch, Vickie stared at him with heated dismay. "Brant—"

"You don't have a problem," he informed her firmly. "I'll watch Mark."

"You!" Vickie gasped.

"I am a responsible adult," he reminded her dryly, amused by the amazement and consternation of her voice.

"But—but, you can't!"

"Why not?"

"Because"—Vickie fumbled for words, watching dazedly as he replaced the phone—"you have to help Smoky in the shop. And I couldn't impose on you."

"I'll take Mark in with me for an hour or so and give him some little task," Brant said, dismissing that protest easily. His hand moved to her elbow and he led her confidently back to the living room. "And it's no imposition. I like kids."

"Listen, Brant, it's nice of you to offer—"

"I'm not offering, I'm doing. Sit down and drink your coffee."

Still dazed, Vickie plopped back onto the divan as he nudged her. A moment later he had stuck her coffee cup into her hands. "Relax!" he ordered her. "I know what I'm doing. Mark will be perfectly safe with me."

"He has to get to bed," Vickie said feebly.

"He will."

"But—" She made one last attempt at refusal, but she was quickly overridden by Brant's stern "No buts. We're lucky this happened now, while *Godspell* is still running. If we were into the run of *Othello*, I couldn't have helped. Now, get that nail out of your mouth before you sever your finger. It's settled."

"All right," Vickie agreed reluctantly. She drained her coffee cup, annoyed when the liquid swished dangerously as her fingers trembled. "I have to take a shower. You can start watching Mark now."

Leaving Brant and her son in the living room, Vickie found herself stomping into the bedroom to collect her things, then stomping into the bathroom and into a cooling shower. She was relieved, but she was also damning Brant to a fiery hell.

What had happened today? She had determined to politely stay as far away from him as possible, but he had rescued her, they had fought, come to a truce, and now he was rescuing her again. He was practically ensconced in her house, and he had gotten himself there with utmost propriety and consideration.

She spoke little as they drove to the theater, a fact that Brant seemed not to notice. Mark was chattering on in his sometimes comprehensible speech.

Fleeing to her dressing room as soon as they reached the stage door, Vickie left explanations for her son's presence up to Brant. He had been so sure everything would be all right, let him handle their mutual employer.

"Spending a lot of time with Mr. Wicker, huh?" Terry quizzed Vickie with lazy, laconic eyes as she slid onto her stool.

"Not really," Vickie replied curtly reaching for her Pan-Cake makeup. Agitated as she was, she didn't feel like dealing with Terry's jibes.

"Oh?" Terry murmured innocently. "Then there's nothing between you?"

"Nothing," Vickie agreed, trying to ignore her.

"Good." Terry swiveled in her chair and watched Vickie's eyes in the bright lights of the mirror. "Then you don't mind if I make a play for him."

Caught off-guard, Vickie froze with her sponge held on the bridge of her nose. Mind? She would mind terribly, she admitted to herself as her heart seemed to take a sudden plunge to her stomach. Frightened as she was of Brant in more ways than one, she knew with a strange ferocity that she would rather be burned by his fire again than watch him in the arms of another woman.

76

She was sure that he had taken lovers in the three years since his departure, but she had never had to see them; they were vague forms of the past. In the last few days while he pursued her, she had convinced herself she didn't want to be caught. But neither did she want him caught, especially by Terry.

"Mind?" Gritting her teeth into a smile, she met Terry's eyes blandly. "Terry, I couldn't stop you from making a play for anyone, could I, whether I minded or not. So"—her eyes narrowed ever so slightly—"go right ahead. Make whatever play you like."

Terry laughed and swept her thick brown hair into a ponytail. "That's true, honey, I will play where I like. But I did want to know where you stood. I'd hate to think that I was the one to keep our little Ice Maiden from thawing."

Vickie rose abruptly, meeting Terry's sweetly devious eyes straight on. "You worry about you, Terry. I'll worry about me."

Terry shrugged and looked back into her own mirror. Vickie wriggled into her costume and left the dressing room, knowing that she was followed by Terry's speculative eyes.

Monte's dinner theater was built like a large, irregular U; the stage, dressing rooms, and dining room occupying the center, the kitchen and food preparation areas to the right, and the costume and stagecraft shops to the left. Taking the latter turn, Vickie decided her hurried makeup session had left her time to check on her son. Entering the huge room that served as the main scene shop, she discovered Mark sitting happily with a paintbrush and an old, out-of-use flat. Brant, looking more like a backwoods logger than famous actor in his worn jeans, Weejuns, and now paintstained flannel shirt, was helping Smoky, Monte's crusty old designer, to saw a stack of lumber into appropriate lengths.

Smoky gave her his absentminded smile and disappeared into the back. Brant switched off his power saw and grinned. "That was a quick change."

Vickie shrugged. "Simple costume, simple makeup. How's it going?" Vickie asked.

"Fine." Brant inclined his head toward Mark, who hadn't noticed his mother. "As you can see." He tugged lightly on one

77

of her pigtails. "Go on, get out of here and have a good show. I promise to take him home soon. Oh, I'll probably stop by my place for a few things. And borrow your shower." He grimaced. "A day of rehearsal and now a fine spray of sawdust. I'm feeling rather rank!"

"Sure," Vickie agreed, covered with a sudden feeling of warmth. It was the same strange warmth she had felt when they were doing the dishes together—a sense of pleasant domesticity she didn't really want to recognize. But as silly as it was, she liked the idea of Brant in her shower. "I'll be home as soon as I can," she said quickly, turning away from him, embarrassed by her thoughts.

"No hurry," he replied cheerfully.

Vickie started down the hall, and then impetuously turned back. Any reservations she had had about leaving Mark with Brant had been problems of her own mind. Brant, looking curiously more macho in his casual clothes than he ever had in a movie, was discussing the fly system for *Othello* with Smoky while still keeping a covert eye on Mark. With that golden lock of hair over an intense blue eye and the breadth of his shoulders emphasized as he crammed his hands into his pockets, his simple presence was hypnotizing, even from a distance. Damn! she told herself disgustedly. She really needed distance! And it was getting harder and harder to keep it.

The show that night went especially well and Vickie was besieged by well-wishers after the curtain call, causing her to run very late. But there was nothing to be done. Monte's, although a popular attraction for tourists, survived because the locals supported it, and every member of the troop knew how very important it was to personally accept praise and congratulations from the audience.

Finally out of costume, Vickie hastily warned Monte that she might need a ride, then ran out to check on her car. Amazingly, it started. She ran back in to inform Monte that she didn't need transportation after all, only to be waylaid as her director decided to tease her.

"Getting chummy with Brant, huh?" Monte demanded with

a feigned solemnity. "For a girl who wouldn't have a drink with him a few nights ago, you seem to be on very good terms."

"You asked to me to be decent," Vickie snapped, tired and wanting only to take her confused emotions home and smother them with sleep.

"Don't go getting temperamental on me!" Monte gasped with mock horror, pretending to be hurt.

"Oh, Lord!" Vickie muttered in disgust, flicking her hair over a shoulder as she strode away. "What I have to put up with to keep a decent job!"

With Monte's laughter ringing behind her, she hurried from the theater to drive home quickly in the sparse late-night traffic. Her house was strangely quiet as she slipped her key into the door.

Walking in, she discovered why. Brant was sound asleep, curled comfortably on the divan, oblivious to his ankles and bare feet, which protruded many inches over the surface. For a moment she stood still and watched him, unable to resist the temptation to study him now in his vulnerable state. The tiny lines around his eyes were faint in repose, the bush of golden hair endearingly disheveled. There was no touch of the quick, dark anger she knew him capable of. He held his slightly parted lips in a half smile, as if his dreams were good ones. Gingerly placing a hand on his shoulder, Vickie could feel his peaceful, even breathing, and the hard muscles that held no tension at rest.

Gnawing afresh on the nail she had started to chew earlier, she stepped away from the divan. It was almost two A.M. It would be a crime to awaken him. In any case, what harm would it be to allow him to finish his night's rest on her divan? She hesitated only a moment longer, then secured a blanket and an extra pillow from her room. Half tenderly and half nervously, she wedged the pillow beneath his head and draped the blanket over his long sprawled-out form. He didn't stir.

With a confused sigh Vickie adjusted the thermostat on the air conditioner, checked on Mark, and turned out the lights. She stopped once more to glance idly at Brant, and to wonder with a wistful curiosity if she did mean anything to him . . . anything at all. Foolish. He was a shining star who loved women and left them. She was an absolute idiot if she ever imagined any more. But very luckily, a very tired idiot. She fell asleep herself almost as soon as her head hit her pillow.

CHAPTER FOUR

"Mommy! Mommy!"

Vickie lifted one protesting eyelid as Mark crawled onto her bed, patting her arm insistently. His little face was ecstatic.

"Brant!" he told her with his excellent pronounciation of the name. "Brant on the couch."

"Yes, I know," Vickie smiled, talking to him as a little adult in the manner she always did. "He was sleeping when I came in, so I left him. Shhhh!"

Mark repeated her motion of putting a finger to her lips.

Still in a state of euphoric half awareness, Vickie glanced longingly back to her cool sheets and plumped pillow. But she didn't want to be caught sleeping when Brant awoke. "Play very quietly," she warned her son, switching off the alarm button which was due to ring any minute, "and Mommy will shower and dress and make breakfast. Then we'll wake Brant, okay?"

Mark nodded happily with his dazzling smile and toddled off to his own room. Grabbing her rehearsal clothing, Vickie flew quickly into the bathroom, determined not to be caught as vulnerable as she had caught Brant the night before. She emerged quickly, but fully dressed, her regular makeup a little more precise than usual.

Totally aware that she was trying to impress Brant, whose motionless form still stretched beneath the blanket—only the tips of his toes and the top of his rumpled head visible—Vickie decided to make a breakfast with all the works, although during the week she and Mark usually settled for toast and cereal. Impressing him, she decided, was not such a terrible desire. She wanted him to leave, thinking her a cool, sophisticated, and competently independent woman.

He finally awoke as the scent of sizzling bacon wafted through the house. Ambling into the kitchen, his hair in fluffy disarray and his eyes still blurred with sleep, he caused Vickie's heart to pound painfully within her chest. He gave her a rueful smile and her breath caught in her throat; her entire body seemed to constrict. Time and wisdom had changed nothing. She loved his rugged, towering frame every bit as much as she had three years ago.

But now, more than then, her feelings and emotions were futile. If there was anything remotely serious in Brant's intentions, there never could be to hers. Out of necessity she had spun a web of deceit between them. A web that must stay at all costs as a wall. A life without Brant breezing through was going to be agony again; it was going to mean sleepless nights and tormented dreams. But a life with Brant knowing about Mark was unthinkable.

"Good morning," she said in a voice unintentionally curt.

"Good morning," he drawled in return, a brow ever so slightly raised in mockery at her tone. He rubbed the back of his neck with both hands. "And yes, thank you, I slept very well."

Vickie hid a flush by giving her undivided attention to the bacon.

"I must say though," Brant continued, helping himself to cup of coffee from the bubbling coffeepot, "that I'm surprised you didn't wake me. It doesn't appear that you're particularly thrilled by my company, and"—he mischievously twitched her fall of hair from her face—"what will the neighbors say?"

"Quit it!" Vickie slapped his hand aside and drained the bacon. "The neighbors won't say anything. I doubt if they'll notice your car, because it's going to drive away with you in it as soon as you've eaten." Transferring the bacon to a plate and grabbing another heaped with fluffy cheese omelettes, Vickie backed out the swinging doors, staring at him. "Grab the toast, please, will you?"

"With pleasure." Brant obediently took the plate and followed

82

Vickie. He refused to acknowledge her withdrawal as they ate, complimenting her profusely and bantering with Mark. When they had finished the meal, he collected his things without argument, apparently willing to leave as directed with no further conversation.

Caught between pain and relief at his easy acquiescence, Vickie was startled when he purposely set his belongings on the chair by the door and took her crudely by the shoulders in a hold that allowed for no escape.

"You know I meant what I said at lunch the other day," he said, his voice as rough and grating as the fingers that held her firmly. "I intend to hound you mercilessly. I am going to have you again, but I'll try to be patient. I want you coming to me, with both of us entirely lucid. There will be no delusions about a rape a second time."

Vickie had met his heated blue gaze with her own eyes steady and she willed them not to lower. She couldn't let him detect the weakness in her.

"Brant," she objected, "I apologized for what I said. But you don't understand. I'm just not interested in an involvement, especially with you."

"Why?" he demanded harshly.

"Because"—she fumbled slightly—"I just don't want you—"

"The hell you don't!" he grated in a low roar. "I kissed you yesterday just to prove that point to myself. And I do believe I proved it."

"Brant—"

Whatever she had been about to say was swiftly torn from her lips. He did not simply kiss her this time; he plundered her mouth with his. He assailed her entire form with his lips and hands, taking complete command of her weakening body. His hands traveled beneath her blouse to tantalize the firm skin of her midriff, then dexterously to unclasp her bra, claiming her breasts under the lace covering with gentle but demanding thoroughness. His fingers massaged the tautening mounds of flesh, drawing patterns that were alternately rough and tender,

83

rubbing his thumbs over her nipples in slightly painful grazes that brought them instantly to full peaks.

Vickie whimpered a protest but, again, he had been so fast. Her arms fell to his, first to attempt to move them, but then to lock there, unwittingly fascinated by the strength and heat beneath them. Despite the jeans they both wore, she could feel his red hot desire burning against her as his hips relentlessly drove into hers. She couldn't move from his arms; she couldn't talk with his mouth sensuously moving over hers, drawing her tongue into the duel she longed to deny but couldn't. It was breathless, whirling, mindless minutes later when she realized she could have spoken, that her lips had been released when he moved his down across her cheek, enticingly circling her ear with moist stabs of his tongue, moving downward again to attack the soft and sensitive flesh of her throat with a demand that was no longer forceful but completely beguiling.

The buttons of her shirt had somehow come undone. His tongue now swept over the areas previously charted by his fingers, nuzzling aside the fabric of her bra with comfortable ease. Primitive excitement whipped through Vickie; it suddenly seemed senseless either to think or talk. The fingers that had pushed at his arms were digging into them, whimpers of protest became whimpers of pleasure. Her hands left his arms to wind around his back, and she was shamelessly pressing herself against him in return, savoring the feel of his overpowering shoulders, breathing in his scent erratically.

Brant's assault stopped abruptly, but where she would have wormed away in acute embarrassment, he held her tightly.

"Why do you lie to me, Vickie?" he whispered, his breath still stimulating as it swept the moistness of her ear. "It's all here, sweetheart. I know that you want me. I believe that you care for me. Why are you afraid?"

He set her an inch away from himself to straighten her clothing, and Vickie wrenched from his grasp. "Would you please just go!" she cried angrily. God! How could she be so easy?

His fists constricted into powerful white knots that matched the tension of his grim lips and severely tightened features. "Yes,

Victoria, I am going. But you can damn well count on the fact that I'll be back. I'm not letting you ruin this for both of us. I don't know what goes on in that secretive little mind of yours, but I promise I will get to the bottom of it. You are afraid of me. I let you off with that cool nonchalance three years ago, but I guarantee I won't again. You became mine on that night when you gave me, I repeat, *gave me,* the virginity you still persist in denying. This time, my love, you're going to stay mine."

"No!" Vickie flared, fumbling with her buttons in her haste to restore herself to order. She couldn't seem to make her fingers work correctly, or drag her eyes from his flaming stare. "I will not be your Sarasota conquest!"

"Is that what it is?" he retorted cruelly. "I think not. If this was just meaningless, as you keep claiming, I don't think you'd give a damn. But as I said, I will have you, and I will get to the bottom of it all."

The door slammed so hard with his departure that the small glass window in it rattled precariously. Shaking stridently as she heard his footsteps click away, Vickie sank to the couch, thinking wildly, going entirely blank, thinking again desperately, her eyes fixed straight ahead, her legs limp.

"Mommy?" Mark's voice calling from his room broke through her numbness.

"Coming," Vickie called, rising absently. "We have to get going, Mark," she continued mechanically.

And then she was angry again. Damn that Brant Wicker for walking back into a life she had carefully glued together from shattered pieces into something workable. Who did he think he was to come back and make demands?

Her anger stayed with her, a sustaining force, as she dropped Mark off at school and drove to the theater.

She arrived a few minutes late to find rehearsal well under way. Sliding into a rear seat beside Terry, who was sullenly sewing a piece of antique lace to a velveteen sleeve, she gave her a surprised, questioning glance.

Terry lifted her shoulders and then dropped them. "Monte's

in one of his moods," she explained in an indifferent whisper. "Who knows? Maybe his cat bit him this morning. He started the minute we began rehearsing. Anyway, I don't suggest you miss any cues." Pushing her own script, which lay on the table before her toward Vickie, Terry warned her, "They're a third of the way through act two. I'd get up there."

"Thanks," Vickie murmured. She opened her own script to the right page, quickly tore through her bag for a pencil, and hurried for the stage, giving Terry a grateful nod. Terry had been right. Monte was indeed in a deplorable mood, lashing out at the slightest mistake. Vickie bit her lips and swallowed the words she wanted to shout back at him, noticing resentfully that Brant seemed to be the only one spared his temper.

But then, she doubted if anyone, even the most influential Hollywood or New York director, would shout at Brant Wicker. He just wasn't the type person one dared to shout at—unless one happened to be a prizefighting gorilla.

Still, Monte was usually pleasant and professional. For him to be acting this way, something had to be wrong. Vickie thought idly that she would question him later; she wasn't about to make a scene in front of the others. Besides, Brant made another entrance as Othello, and Monte started to mellow. By the time Brant and Vickie exited together, neither Monte's burst of irascibility nor the intensity of temper in which Brant had left Vickie's house seemed to have ever existed.

She pulled out of Brant's hold the second their footsteps took them into the wings, but he made no attempt to stop her. Instead, she could hear his chuckle following her as she slithered offstage away from him. He stayed behind, and she wished fervently that she could walk back and rail at him, informing him that her hasty retreat had not been because of him, and her supposed fear of him, but because she wanted to talk to Monte. That, of course, wouldn't be entirely true. She did want to quiz Monte in private and tell him his behavior had been atrocious. But more than that, she did want to get away from Brant.

"What was that all about?" Vickie demanded of Monte as soon as the scene ended and a five-minute break was called.

Monte tossed his pencil on the table and leaned back in his chair. "Nothing," he told her disgustedly. "Absolutely nothing, do you believe that?" He stood and stretched. "No reason, no excuse, except that I'm tired." Looking at her with a puzzled smile, he continued. "I'm sorry, Vickie. Excuse me, now I have to go say I'm sorry to everyone else!"

Bobby sank into the chair Monte had occupied a second after he had left. Vickie glanced at him questioningly, since it was obvious he had sought her out.

"So, love," he asked, "have a nice night?"

Vickie's brows angled into arches. "I don't know," she replied dryly. "You seem to be in on something I'm not. *Did* I have a nice night?"

"Sweet and innocent to the end!" Bobby proclaimed, chuckling. "I am inquiring with all concern for your welfare. You and our gallant leading man, it appears, have become the 'in' thing. How brokenhearted I was! I drove by your house this morning to make sure you had a ride in, since Monte told me you were having car trouble. And what do I find? My virgin princess, my pedestal queen, involved in a normal, mortal relationship. Spending the night with Brant Wicker!"

"Oh, Lord!" Vickie snapped. "I did not spend the night with Brant!"

"Oh? He just happened to stop by at seven A.M.?"

"Of course not!"

"Then he did spend the night at your place?"

Vickie sighed. The question, from Bobby, was motivated by genuine concern. She and Bobby had long ago formed a strong bond of friendship, and they usually discussed just about anything—mostly Bobby's love problems. The tables were merely turned now.

"Yes. No. I mean, yes, Brant did sleep at my house. But, no, we're not sleeping together. He watched Mark last night, and when I came in, he was sleeping. So I left him alone." Her simple explanation—an easy one to Bobby—would possibly involve other repercussions. "Don't say anything to anyone else please, huh, Bob. I'm not up to the teasing."

Bobby sighed flatly and patted her hand. "Sorry, kid, you're already in for the teasing. I didn't say anything. I consider any of my information about your life classified information. But Connie happened to drive by to check on you, too, and you might as well have printed the story on the front page of the newspaper. I'm sure she's told half the cast, if not half the city already."

"Damn!" Vickie moaned, bitterly remembering her thought that allowing Brant to sleep on her sofa could cause no harm. "Damn!"

Bobby was right. If not actually giving her a ribald comment, every member of the cast at least sent knowing, furtive glances her way. Brant, she noticed, was oblivious to it all. Of course, he would be, she thought angrily. No one would think of throwing taunts in his direction.

She cornered Brant in the wing while they blocked the third scene for the day. "I'd appreciate it," she told him sternly, "if you would help me dispel the rumors floating around."

"What rumors?" he asked, puzzled.

An annoying blush rose to her cheeks. "Your car was seen by a certain party with a news-spread larger than that of the *National Enquirer.*"

"Ahhh," he murmured. "So you're being ribbed about sleeping with me."

"Precisely!" Vickie grated.

"Pity it's only a rumor at the moment," Brant mused.

"Brant!"

"Don't fret," he advised. "It won't be long."

"You really are a cocky bastard!" Vickie hissed, ready to explode.

"No, Vickie, I'm sorry. But don't you think you're overreacting a bit? What the hell should you care what anyone is saying? Lord, Vickie, you're of legal age. What you do or don't do is your own business. If you don't like a certain rumor, ignore it!"

With her irritation put into a new context, Vickie realized that she was falling right into the hands of those who wished to torment her. Deflated, Vickie glanced around the dim wing to see that her tone had brought curious eyes to them. Riveting her attention back to Brant, she saw the depths of amusement her discomfiture was causing him in the wicked blue gleam of his eyes. Lowering her whisper to a barely discernible sound, she muttered, "This isn't funny."

"Sorry." He cupped a hand to his ear and leaned toward her. "I missed what you said."

"Damn you!"

"What's that? I'm a lamb?"

"Cute."

"Sorry," he repeated, "but don't expect me to get upset. I do find it all amusing, and so would you if you allowed yourself a sense of humor."

"Listen, Mr. Hotshot Movie Star," Vickie denounced him, "rumors are funny in Hollywood. Maybe in New York, maybe even in Tampa or Jacksonville. This is Sarasota. I have a son—"

"Oh, hell, Vickie. This is twentieth-century Sarasota. Besides, your son is going to have a new father before he knows what a rumor is. I said I intend to have you, and I meant all the way. I'm going to marry you too."

She didn't have a chance to say or do anything except gasp. In a single string of dialogue, he went on to excuse himself and move to the edge of the stage where she watched his metamorphosis into Othello.

He was insane. No, he was joking.

But he was, indeed, a superb actor. As Vickie joined him onstage at her cue, he quickly had her immersed in the magic illusion of acting with the special fervor he seemed to draw from them all. It was easy to be Desdemona, easy to give him the unshakable love the role demanded, easy to fear him. Brant, minus costume, makeup, and set, could hypnotize all his fellow players.

Vickie felt almost bereft when she walked offstage. Forcing her drained body down the side apron steps, she unobtrusively took a seat near Monte. Quietly, so as not to disturb the director's concentration, she poured herself a cup of coffee from the gold restaurant carafe upon the table. Sipping the hot brew, she felt its warmth revitalize her. Brant was sapping her of strength, onstage and off. Usually so self-assured, she was at a complete loss on how to handle him. For now, she was going to have to ignore him.

When he finally came offstage, she sipped her coffee and studied her script without looking up. He wasn't bothered in the least. His attention went convivially to a few of the others—Terry, among them—who were all too happy to include him in their discourse. Covertly, and with a stab of jealousy she despised, Vickie saw that Terry was still anxious to make her play for Brant, rumors or no. The tall brunette was unabashedly draped over him as she whispered a question intently, and damn Brant if he didn't turn to give her a dazzling smile.

"Hold it just a minute," Monte told them all, leaping to the stage. "I think I've got one of those impossible to refuse offers—in the form of an apology! I know I was horrible today. I'm tired. So you must be tired too. Sooooooo—we're dark Sunday and Monday. I'm giving you Tuesday daytime off. No rehearsal. Just report for showtime. For those of you who wish to make it, I'm also extending an open invitation. I've rented a place up in the panhandle for the weekend. The beach, sun, and sailboats. If you can't make it, relax somehow! That's it. See you all tonight."

"Dynamite!" Bobby murmured beside Vickie, giving her a pleased grin. "Two fun-filled days on old Monte! You gonna go, Vick?"

"I'm not sure," she hedged. "I have Mark to think about—"

"Now, that's pure bunk," Monte proclaimed, interrupting them, wryly astounding Vickie with his ability to hear what he wanted to hear. "I happen to know for a fact that you can easily leave Mark. You told me yourself just last week that your parents and your brother have been hounding you about having Mark spend some time with them. And you, Victoria, have been almost as grouchy as I. If anyone needs a vacation, it's you."

She needed a vacation all right, but away from the theater and its newest star. And she was sure beyond a doubt that Brant would be going.

"Maybe," she hedged again, determined to make no commitments. "It's just that I see so little of Mark myself."

"We're talking about two days, not two weeks," Monte reminded her.

Vickie gave both Monte and Bobby a cheerful smile that didn't quite reach her eyes. "Maybe," she repeated cheerily. "Probably, even!" Let them both think she was going. The less time they had to chisel at her defenses, the better.

Glancing over Monte's graying head, she saw that Brant was leisurely approaching their party. Her smile became deceptively dazzling as she hopped quickly to her feet. "I've got to run. See you all later."

Spinning around, she made a graceful if hasty exit from the theater. Knowing Brant, he would find a way to trick her into agreement to the weekend. Or would he? Would he really care whether she went or not? He hadn't appeared too unhappy to have Terry draped over him and Terry had made it bluntly clear that she enjoyed draping herself.

Later that afternoon, sitting on the divan, she found it hard to concentrate on her lines, easy as they should have been to learn. Her mind kept wandering back to Brant's words. *I plan to marry you.* How absurd. He probably hadn't really given her a thought in the years preceding his reappearance. His words were merely Hollywood and New York, she thought scornfully. In those sophisticated cities, talk was cheap, at least in the theatrical community. Light affairs were easy. They were easy anywhere, she told herself dryly, except that it was true. You could read about many a famous actor's marriage one week, and his divorce the next, which didn't matter. All she could ever have with Brant would be an affair. She couldn't marry him even if he were serious. Marriage meant licenses, and if they applied for a license, Brant would discover that she was not a widow.

"No!" she voiced aloud to herself. "Damn you, Brant Wicker. Not again!"

"Brant!" Mark, who had been quietly playing with a set of Bristle Blocks, looked up at the name and repeated it with a smile. "Brant coming?"

"No, no, darling," Vickie said quickly. "Mommy was just thinking aloud."

Just thinking aloud. Ridiculous. There was no future in dreaming. Better to subdue immediately the dreams that could never be. Not with the obstacles that faced them—the main one of which Brant would never dream.

She never intended to ask anyone to watch Mark for Monte's two-day holiday because she didn't intend to go. As it happened, though, Edward called her a few minutes before she was due to leave for the evening's performance. Inadvertently she mentioned Monte's plans, explaining that she had a few days off if Edward thought they might be able to get together.

"No!" Edward told her emphatically over the wire. "We are not going to get together. You're going to go with your group and have a good time. I'll take Mark. Listen, young lady," he added firmly before she could protest, "you are one of the best mothers I know. But you have to have a life of your own too. A one-dimensional parent is not good! Besides, Mark needs a little male companionship, and who better than his doting uncle?"

Vickie had to chuckle at her brother's tone, and agree. Edward had shown a poignant devotion to Mark since his birth. He had stood beside her from the beginning, a shoulder to lean on when the going had been rough. Karen, Edward's new wife, was also crazy about her little dark-headed nephew.

As Edward went on to give her a host of reasons why she should go and Mark should stay with him, Vickie felt her resolve melting.

She was going to be with Brant for the summer; to deny herself the little vacation to avoid him was ludicrous.

"Okay, okay!" she finally agreed laughingly. "Thanks, Ed. I could use the days at Monte's expense! When do you want to pick up Mark?"

Her brother told her he would pick up Mark on Saturday morning, and after a few more minutes of idle chatter about their parents and their jobs, they hung up.

Vickie had barely seated herself on her stool in the dressing room that night before a sharp knock sounded on the door. The women looked at one another. "Probably Monte," Terry said dryly, rising to answer the door. "Hope he's still in his good mood."

It wasn't Monte. Brant's towering form stood in the doorway, rigid with ill-concealed anger. "Welcome, big boy—" Terry began, but he cut her off shortly with a curt nod.

"Vickie, I'd like to talk to you before you go on," he said tonelessly, only his stance and searing eyes betraying his emotions. Spinning on his heel and stiffly striding away, he was gone before she could open her mouth to protest or assent, taking her agreement imperiously for granted.

"My, my," Connie murmured, her huge brown eyes wide and full of alarm. "What on earth did you do to him?"

"Nothing," Vickie replied shortly, stunned, but determined to show no reaction to Brant's high-handedness. Inside she was seething with fury and indignation, but with three pairs of eyes staring at her with curiosity, she had to pretend total indifference. Picking up her sponge, she calmly began to apply base to her cheeks. Eventually the other women lowered their eyes. Only Terry stared straight ahead at her own mirror, a secret smile curved into her lips.

"How dare you barge into the dressing room and speak to me like that?" Vickie demanded after she had sought Brant out and found him in the scene shop laboriously pounding nails. "Just who do you think you are?"

The hammer paused in mid-air and Brant swiveled slowly toward her, his eyes still burning darkly. For a terrified instant he reminded Vickie of a lord from the Renaissance—an all-powerful master who might easily bludgeon an erring female. But then the hammer fell innocently to his side. His voice was his weapon, lashing out with the strength of a whip.

"Who do I think I am?" he thundered in a rasp. "Nothing much. A fellow human being, currently a fellow member of this ensemble." Dropping the hammer with a clanging thud to the cold cement floor, he strode angrily to a rough-hewn workbench to pick up a pile of several newspapers. Stamping furiously back

93

to Vickie, he thrust them into her hands. "These are what I want to talk to you about."

Vickie still had no conception of what he could be ranting about. "Those are newspapers," she drawled sarcastically, stating the obvious and infuriating him further.

"Read the circled articles," Brant commanded.

Brant had maintained his grip on the papers even as he had thrust them into Vickie's unwilling hands. Now she looked at him heatedly and jerked them from his grasp, her gray eyes as stormy and as cold as his blue ones. Finally allowing her vision to take in the newspapers, Vickie saw immediately that the publications were major ones from across the country. And the circled articles were about Brant, told to the reporters by a nameless but well-known "leading lady of the Central Florida troupe."

Vickie's heart sank slowly as she briefly scanned the articles. They were damaging, to say the least. Still, she was certain that Brant's anger didn't stem from the temperamental portrayal given of him, but from the fact that his private life—one he had always kept from the media—had been ripped wide open. Every personal piece of information imaginable had been given, down to his present address. And to make matters worse, it was even hinted that a romantic entanglement "destined to end at the altar" was going on between the star and the leading lady who had been so helpful to the papers.

Vickie was horrified as she met Brant's accusing stare, and equally filled with wrath.

"I don't care what this looks like!" she sputtered in a vengeful hiss. "I didn't give this interview!"

"I didn't accuse you yet."

"No?" Vickie countered. "Then why am I standing here?"

"I'm asking you," Brant said more calmly. "If you didn't give the interview, it was certainly intended to look as if you did. You do have all this information."

"All right, I do!" Vickie fumed as she tried to remain steadfastly cool and in control. "But I didn't have anything to do with this. And I'm not going to stand here giving you excuses. Look

94

for your culprit elsewhere." Belying her words, she remained planted before him, hands defiantly on her hips, gray eyes blazing into indigo for a sign that he believed her.

But signs were sometimes impossible to read from Brant. He stood as still as she, white-knuckled fists clenched in his pockets. With the angle of his arms emphasizing broad shoulders that trimmed to slender hips encased in jeans that hugged and visibly displayed the muscles in his legs beneath the fabric, he again reminded her of some fearsome warlord of another century. A Viking, a savage chieftain. Othello the Moor, about to commit murder over an imagined wrong.

"You don't have to give me excuses," he said grimly. "I was merely asking. If you say you know nothing about it, I believe you."

Stunned by his words, Vickie stood still in disbelief. "You have one hell of a way of just asking!"

"I'm annoyed."

"*Annoyed?*"

"Okay. I'm rather irate. I can't imagine anyone doing something like this to me."

"Terrific. So you turn to me."

"I'm sorry. I also intend to turn elsewhere. Got any ideas?"

Vickie hardened her jaw as she clenched her teeth. She had an idea—a damned good one. But she didn't intend to voice it, certainly not when she didn't trust his look. He said that he believed her, but did he really?

"Brant, these are newspaper articles. Anyone can talk. There are at least twenty people around here who could have come up with any of this."

The stark anger left his eyes for a moment of puzzlement. "But why would anyone want to hurt me?" he mused.

"I don't think anyone did intend to hurt you," Vickie said quietly.

"What are you talking about? I'll be besieged at home if I don't move now! Whoever did this even gave out my parents' address in Tampa! They are not young people. They don't need the harassment they're going to get—"

95

"The pain of notoriety!" Vickie interrupted dryly. "You're a star. Surely you've been maligned before."

"Not by supposed friends."

"Oh, it was a friend, all right," Vickie muttered beneath her breath.

"What?" Brant demanded sharply.

"Nothing. Nothing I can't handle myself," she murmured. "Excuse me, that is if the third degree is over. I do have a show tonight." Majestically spinning on him, she sailed out of the shop and down the hall to the wings, not sure whom she'd rather give a sound slap to first—Brant, for believing her capable of being so petty, or Terry, who she was convinced had given the interview and purposely set it up to appear that Vickie had.

Vickie reached the wing just in the nick of time to hear Jim bellow his "places" command. And as the show proceeded, she decided that acting was a wonderful thing. Her head was in a turmoil as vicious as any raging storm, but her lines came out ringing sincerity. Only in the wings during the act breaks was she unusually subdued, wondering what to do.

If she really wanted to get rid of Brant, this was her chance. But she knew damn well that Terry, determined to get Brant, had given the interview. She couldn't sit by and have Brant, who had professed to believe her, harbor suspicions in the back of his mind. Pride, she told herself, goeth before the fall . . . In any event she wasn't letting Terry get away with it and sit idly by.

As she broodingly mused, Terry sauntered over to her. "Anything wrong? she asked solicitously. "Macho-man get your dander up?"

"No, Terry," Vickie drawled calmly, watching the pretty brunette. "But you might say that I am a little irritated."

"Oh? I did hear that you and Brant were shacking up. If you've had a little lovers' quarrel, perhaps I can help," Terry offered.

"Brant and I are not shacking up," Vickie explained, the terminology bothering her more than Terry's attitude. "And I'm not irritated with Brant. Quite frankly, Terry, I'm irritated with you."

"Me!" The brunette feigned a pained innocence.

"Come on, Terry," Vickie retorted. "I'm not one of your drooling dates. Haven't you read the papers? Your interviews were well received."

For an instant Terry's sultry eyes flashed something like a fearful defiance. Then they clouded. "I don't know what you're talking about. We all give interviews all of the time."

"Oh, but these are especially good," Vickie told her caustically.

"Perhaps someone twisted what I said—"

"Places!" Tim's command broke off further conversation.

Whispering quickly as she moved to her assigned space, Vickie warned Terry, "Perhaps you'd better tell Brant that your words were twisted. . . ."

Terry did tell Brant with an acting ability Vickie had as yet to see on a stage. She watched only a few minutes of the little scenario. Terry caught Brant offstage right after the curtain fell at the end of *Godspell*. There had never been such an abject display of feminine remorse. And Terry came off as the maligned one, her innocent words misused and abused. As she spoke to Brant, her long, lacquered fingernails resting lightly on his shoulder with her emphatic sincerity, Vickie turned away. She was in the clear herself, but she didn't want to see Brant's understanding forgiveness of Terry. It wasn't fair. She had taken the brunt of his temper. Terry had merely to wind herself around him and—men! Surely Brant couldn't be that idiotic! So much for his being "a little bit in love" with her.

Suddenly Vickie was tired. The tension she had been living with was draining her. Rushing into the dressing room, she scrubbed her face and changed, in a hurry to leave, not interested in another encounter with either Brant or Terry.

But if she had hoped to avoid Brant, she was sadly disappointed. As she hastened to the parking lot, she found him waiting for her, leaning against her Volvo.

"What now?" she flashed angrily. "Did someone break your board? Put nails in your tires? Throw salt in your coffee?"

"None of the above!" he laughed, languidly straightening himself. "I want to apologize."

"Terrific, you've apologized," she said coolly, inserting her key into the lock. "Now, if you'll excuse me . . ."

"It won't start." He moved around the car to grin into her window.

"What?" she demanded, annoyed, punching the key into the ignition.

"I said it won't start, but if you don't want to take my word for it, try it!" He continued to grin at her, leaning confidently on the frame. Vickie gave him a nasty glare and turned the key. Nothing. Spewing forth a barrage of venomous words, she pushed his elbow away from the car, opened the door, and sprang from the vehicle to further emphasize her wrath. "And you had the nerve to accuse me of that interview! Brant Wicker, you are a—"

"Hell of a nice guy, really," he finished, halting her vengeful fury by slipping one arm securely around her back and using the other to bring his hand to her mouth and clamp it shut, laughing until her futile struggles ceased. Without releasing his hold, he calmly informed her, "There's nothing really wrong with your car. A loose wire. I found it when I fixed it for you the other night. Come to think of it, you never did say thanks, but that's all right, don't mention it. I loosened the same wire. I was afraid you'd try to run off instead of listening to me. What's that?" he asked as she made a muffled comment into his hand. "Sounds like 'let me go.' Not yet. I want to make sure you've calmed down a bit! Oh, brother! Here comes Harry Blackwell. Let's not have him see us arguing." His hand slipped from her mouth, but even as she gulped for air, his mouth replaced it, searing into hers hungrily, passionately. One hand now held her to him securely around her lower back, the other reinforced his conquering command by pinning her to him by her nape. Stiffening, she strained against him, unable to fight, unable even to lift an arm. Suddenly she didn't want to. The scent of his light, musky cologne mingled in her nostrils with an aura that was all him, all masculine, all seductive. The pounding of his heart was as clear to her ears as her own, as his lips possessed her and his tongue parted her quivering mouth—searching, probing, demanding. Sensing her surrender, he eased his deathlike grip and his hands began to wander, caressing the small of her back, teasing her ribs, moving along the smooth, alabaster skin of her neck, down to her collarbone, down briefly to cradle the curves of her breasts before they locked again behind her back to allow his lips to follow the same course.

Sanity finally sprang to her mind. "Brant, let me go!" Her attempt at reproachful scorn came out more like pathetic subjugation, but he released her immediately and she almost fell to the concrete in weak surprise. "Sure," he said with a devilish chuckle, "you sound much calmer now, and Harry is halfway down the street."

"I am anything but calm! I am furious. Irate. Inflamed—" Her voice was growing louder with each expletive. Grabbing her wrist, Brant's fingers completely encircling it, he marched the few spaces to his own car, dragging her behind him. Her knees were still too rubbery to resist; she couldn't find the air to vocalize a protest. He opened the driver's door and propelled her in, following so closely that she was forced to move or be crushed by his steel-hard frame. He slammed the door, inserted the key into the ignition, and pulled out onto the highway, all before she could utter a word. Incredulous, strangling with indignation, she finally garbled a harsh, "What on earth do you think you're doing?"

He shrugged pleasantly. "I'm trying to talk to you."

"Talk! You weren't talking! You attacked me!"

"I did not!" He gave her a grimace of feigned shock. "Well, maybe for just a minute. But all's fair in love and war, as they say. So I'm glad I made the attack. I won the skirmish."

"You didn't win a thing," she protested angrily.

"Yes, I did," he replied with firm simplicity, pulling his eyes from the road to glance her way for a second. What she saw in them in that split-second sent alternating flows of chilling ice water and boiling lava through her veins. His eyes weren't brilliant with laughter or dark with rough-cut anger. They were clear, crystal-clear with pointed determination and something else she couldn't quite discern, a shade far more dangerous than any she was familiar with already. Taking a deep breath, she decided to change her tactics. "Brant, I have to get home," she said softly.

"I'm taking you home."

"My car . . ."

"I'll pick you up in the morning."

So much for her new tactics. "Damn you, Brant Wicker! You've been playing too many roles! You can't drive me around against my will. We are not living in Shakespearean days! You have no power over me; you can't control me!"

"Obviously I can!" Brant chuckled dryly. "But don't worry, I don't intend to often! You'll shortly be controlling yourself— my way."

"You have gone stark raving mad!" Vickie charged him, inching as far as she could from his compelling warmth to keep her words aloof. She leaned against the door as she eyed him skeptically and added, "But don't worry. I'm sure you'll find a production of *One Flew over the Cuckoo's Nest* somewhere, and fit right in."

He laughed easily and glanced her way with a patronizing smile curling the full lips, whose sensual touch she could still feel upon her own. "Snapping at me isn't going to change a thing."

"What is there to change?" Vickie demanded with exasperation.

"Us."

"There is no 'us,'" Vickie objected calmly, but unable to resist, she added, "Don't you think you should be having this conversation with Terry? I'll bet she'd be just as receptive to your advances as you were to her apology."

"Do I detect a hidden note of jealousy?" Brant queried with a lifted brow, his eyes on the deserted highway.

"No." Vickie lied. "Simple fact."

"I was not receptive to Terry. I know exactly what she was doing. Do you take me for a complete idiot?" He glanced at her with his mouth forming a thin line.

100

Vickie shrugged. The idea had occurred to her.

"I had to accept her apology," Brant continued curtly. "I could hardly challenge her with a right hook to her jaw."

"You weren't suffering through the apology," Vickie said dryly.

In the flickering light of a streetlamp, Vickie saw his features tighten. "I don't care what Terry does. I do care about what you do."

"Wonderful. So I get the right hook to the jaw," Vickie snapped bitterly.

"Damn it, Victoria. I said I was sorry."

"So Brant Wicker says he's sorry and all is okay," Vickie murmured.

"Self-righteous, aren't you?" Brant countered coolly.

Vickie's murky lashes fluttered and fell. Maybe she was, but she was always on the defensive, always wondering. She battled mental demons he couldn't begin to imagine and, admittedly, she still resented him. She had had a child alone. She had battled for two years by herself to make a worthwhile life.

But suddenly the long-ago decision she had to keep Mark's birth a secret didn't seem so right. Looking at Brant covertly, at the firm and rugged strength of his jaw, she shivered slightly. He would not consider her deception right. He would consider it self-righteous. God only knew what his reaction would be if he ever learned the extent of her deceit.

A tangled web. She had started off lying, and now the lies had to go on, meshing into finer and finer threads that seemed to strangle her while others went on unaware.

"Brant," she said. "Let's just forget it. I have to get home."

"I am taking you home."

"My car—"

"I'll pick you up in the morning."

Vickie clamped her mouth shut. She was too tired to argue futilely over transportation at the moment. In the morning she would be more up to handling him. Allowing her head to sink into the high, comfortably plush backrest of the car, Vickie closed her eyes. It would be so easy to open her eyes and discover

101

that everything was a dream. But when her eyes opened, they did so with alarm. The Mercedes had taken a swift turn off the road and onto the embankment, and Brant had switched off the engine and was staring at her with dark mischief in his eyes.

"Oh, no," Vickie grumbled, returning his stare suspiciously. "What now? I have a son at home, and a baby-sitter still nursing an injured hand. I have to get home!"

"I am getting you home," Brant replied, and his smile went surprisingly soft as he watched her. Her hair, released from the restraining pigtails of her *Godspell* character, fluffed about her face, the deep inky black matching the thick lashes shading her tired gray eyes. Her lips were enticingly red against the creaminess of her fine features, but he refrained from touching them. She could elicit a throbbing flame of passion from him with a single glance, but that passion was now held in check by a deep-rooted tenderness. Brant knew a barrier rose between them; Vickie was capable of being a glacial wall of steadfast reserve, but he had seen cracks in that wall, and he was determined to gently tear the entire thing down.

"I am taking you home," he repeated softly, touching a tendril of the pitch black hair with a lightness that was almost reverence. "But first you're going to promise to drive up to the panhandle with me."

She was immediately on the alert, jerking from the headrest. "Brant, I'm not even sure if I'm going—"

"Liar!" he charged in impatient interruption. "I know you're going. Bobby mentioned that your brother is taking Mark."

Vickie sat silently for a moment while Brant leisurely crossed his arms and emitted a sigh of resignation, settling back into the car. "Hey," he murmured, "I can sit here all night. The stars are out; it's a beautiful view."

"All right, all right!" Vickie half laughed and half wailed her agreement out without conscious thought.

"Promise?"

"Promise."

"I'll hold you to it," he warned, the blue of his eyes an intense violet in the night. "There will be an abduction if you try to back out on me."

"I won't," Vickie said softly.

The Mercedes geared back into life. They were both quiet as they drove the few remaining blocks to Vickie's house. She was dazed by her own acquiescence, staring at the white-gold splendor of his head caught in the play of the moonbeams, not thinking yet of consequences.

He left her at her door with the briefest of good-night kisses, his lips barely brushing hers. But still their touch seemed ingrained. . . .

Vickie managed a few minutes of polite, idle conversation with Mrs. Gimball, then locked the door wearily when the sitter left before walking into the bedroom to check on her son. He was at complete peace as he slept, his lids lightly shuttering his blue eyes, his breathing tranquil. So like his father. . . .

Turning, Vickie walked into her own room and lay on the bed without bothering to undress. Like a wavering moth, she was moving closer and closer to a flame. But she couldn't deny that the flame existed, or that she was actually willing to be scorched again just to feel its warmth one more time, for however brief a spell.

CHAPTER FIVE

If she lived to be one hundred, Vickie decided she would never understand Brant Wicker. After literally abducting her and holding her prisoner—if being swept into a Mercedes and held by a roadside for five minutes could be considered abduction and imprisonment—he spent the rest of the week practically ignoring her. He was polite and cordial, occasionally seeking her out, but no more so than any other cast member.

Confused, Vickie didn't know what to think. She should be grateful, but she had finally decided to accept carefully whatever the summer had to offer. Mechanisms in her mind warned that she could never really have Brant Wicker for so many reasons that they made her head spin. But just as surely as she knew the limitations, she knew she wanted whatever she could have.

Which was nothing, she began to think as Saturday morning rolled around with no further word from Brant. Nothing but pure torture.

Edward appeared for Mark about a half hour before the scheduled time, grinning at her doorstep and demanding she sit down with him for a cup of coffee to fill him in on the latest at the theater. Grinning in return at her tall, gaunt brother, Vickie affectionately pulled him into the house by a large-boned hand. Edward was gray-eyed and raven-haired like his sister, but none of his mother's—or more recently his wife's—efforts had ever put meat on his frame. He was too thin to really be a handsome man, but his eyes were deep with expression and sincerity, and when he smiled, which he often did, his face was lit with the beauty of an innate intelligence and compassion. Life did have its wonderful aspects; a brother like Edward was one of them.

"So who is the star this summer?" Edward demanded as he stirred milk into his coffee and made himself at home at Vickie's sunny yellow kitchen table.

Vickie glanced at her brother with some surprise and then quickly averted her eyes, pouring herself a cup of coffee. "Haven't you read the papers?"

"Not in the last few days," Edward answered regretfully. In the process of turning his hobby and love, tropical fish, into a full-scale business, Edward was often much busier than he would like to be. "So tell me, our man must be a biggie if he's making all the papers."

"Brant Wicker," Vickie told him casually.

Edward let out a long whistle. "That *is* big stuff! Back to his humble beginnings, huh?"

Vickie shrugged and sipped at her coffee. "He is one man I'd like to meet," Edward continued. "I've always been impressed by him. He had one hell of a service record, you know."

"Did he?" Vickie inquired politely, wishing she could change the subject without being too obvious.

"Ummm . . ." Edward began to ramble on about Brant's past and Vickie suddenly decided to wipe down already sparkling counters while pretending to listen with interest and praying something would happen to halt her brother's adulation.

Something did happen. The doorbell started to ring.

"Probably Bobby, come to cajole breakfast out of me!" Vickie told Edward cheerfully, escaping briefly to the living room, but Edward sauntered close behind her.

Mark looked up from a pile of toy soldiers to helpfully inform her, "Door, Mommy."

Vickie smiled at him wryly. "Thanks, Mark." Glad of the interruption, she quickly swung open the door only to freeze with dismay. Brant had chosen his moment to reappear.

"May I come in?" he drawled with amusement as she gaped at him, stunned.

"I suppose," she murmured warily, her manner not particularly gracious as she backed away from the door.

"Brant!" Mark threw down his toys and toddled swiftly on chubby legs toward the blond giant, annoying Vickie with his eagerness. However, no one was paying her the slightest attention. Mark and Brant were involved with themselves, Edward was gaping by the swinging kitchen doors, his expression much like his sister's as she had thrown open the door.

Recovering, Vickie jolted herself into a modicum of decorum. "Brant, I'd like you to meet my brother, Edward. Ed, this is Brant Wicker."

Brant looked from Mark, whom he had hoisted into his arms, with an amiable curiosity to meet the man standing in the hall. A pleasant smile lit his angular features and he strode to Edward with a hand outstretched. Once more, Vickie thought with a pang, it was easy to understand Brant's personal popularity. He was fire; he was ice. But most of all, he was a man. His magnificent body held an assured arrogance, but he offered himself to others completely, treating those he met with an instant respect that created an overwhelming and immediate loyalty to him.

She could see acceptance in her brother's eyes as the two men shook hands. And then she saw something else. Puzzlement. Edward looked like a man who had the answer to a crossword puzzle right on the tip of his tongue but just couldn't get it. And yet if he stayed long enough . . . if he had a chance to really compare eyes . . . Edward already knew full well that there was no Mr. Langley.

Knowing that she had to get rid of her brother, Vickie sputtered to life. "Brant, we were just having coffee, would you like a cup? Edward has to leave right away; his wife is waiting for him and Mark."

"Sure, I'd love coffee," Brant agreed comfortably. "It's a pity your brother has to go."

"I don't—" Edward began.

"You do!" Vickie insisted, trying to feign a sisterly message that said she wanted to be alone with Brant. Unfortunately

106

Edward knew her well; an unhappy suspicion of something was forming on his gaunt features.

"I suppose I do have to get back," Edward said, watching his sister and emitting messages as she had. His voice had a little harshness to it, and she knew that he was wondering just what she was up to.

Although he had stood by her, Edward had never approved of her not telling Mark's father that he had a son. He felt strongly that a man had a right to know he had a child—and that he also had a duty toward that child, no matter what the differences between the parents. Still, Edward was her brother. She wasn't afraid that he would purposely betray her, but if he did put two and two together and come up with four, guilt would riddle his face. He was incapable of deceit. Brant would surely become suspicious.

Fighting an almost overwhelming panic, Vickie called upon every reserve of training and poise to behave nonchalantly as she hurried Edward through his coffee and ushered him and Mark out the door, almost forgetting she wouldn't be seeing her son for two days. It was Brant's hug for the boy that reminded her, and she cradled Mark to her tenderly, reminding herself that he was truly the most important thing in her life.

Brant stood in the driveway waving with Vickie until Edward's Toronado was out of sight. Then, uneasily, Vickie realized that his piercing stare was boring into her back.

"What was that all about?" he demanded point blank.

Whipping around to meet the fathomless blue ice of his eyes, Vickie shrugged innocently. "What was what all about?"

"Why were you practically throwing your brother out of the house?"

"His wife is waiting," Vickie replied without blinking, despising the fact that it was becoming so easy to lie without faltering. Knowing she wouldn't be able to meet the cool opaque of his eyes for long, she swept past Brant and back into the house, knowing he followed her on his deceptively soft tread, but she braced herself for any further questions.

But there weren't any and he made her increasingly nervous

as he stood watching her collect cups, his wiry form exuding an unsettling energy that was as vibrant as sunlight despite the casual way he was leaning against the refrigerator. She had the prickly feeling that he might pounce upon her at any second and render her as helpless as a small child by his sheer force and indomitable willpower. But he made no move and she finally reached a state where she turned on him to snap, "What do you want anyway?"

His brows arched in sardonic surprise. "What do I want? Just the pleasure of your company. You did agree to drive north with me."

Vickie washed a saucer for the second time. "The panhandle isn't until tomorrow," she said cautiously, torn between a desire to be with him and the near fanatical fear left her by her brother's almost discovering the truth.

"I know. But I thought we'd drive up tonight after the show."

Vickie's hands froze on the plate. She felt a shiver within her, for she knew her answer would be significant in their relationship. She could be jumping from the frying pan into the fire, and yet she wasn't jumping, she was somehow being pushed.

As if from a great distance, she heard her own voice incredibly indifferent. "All right, if that's what you want to do. I believe the drive is several hours."

Brant grimaced. "It's not all that bad. If we can leave the theater by midnight, we'll reach the beach house by three."

Vickie started as she found the saucer being patiently tugged from her hand and the running spigot being turned off. "I really do think that that thing is clean—sterile enough for a newborn," Brant said dryly. "Why in hell are you so frightened of me?"

Denial rose immediately to her lips. "I'm not frightened of you."

But she was, more so than ever with him hovering over her. She was tall, but the top of her head merely came to his chin, his aggressive masculinity an aura that engulfed her. And the look in his eyes—tender, compassionate, protectively curious— was far more frightening than even his anger. God help me, she

108

thought, tilting her head proudly, don't let him push now because I don't think I can handle it.

But Brant didn't push. "Okay," he said agreeably, putting both hands on her slender shoulders and firmly leading her out of the kitchen, "you're not afraid of me. Good. Then go get dressed."

"For what?" Vickie asked, noting suddenly that he was wearing a superbly tailored lightweight leisure suit that enhanced the clean lines of his trim, broad-shouldered build.

"We're going to lunch."

"But we're leaving tonight!"

"So? If I'm planning on marrying you shortly, I have to get in a few dates first."

Annoyed, Vickie planted her feet firmly on the ground and faced him. "I wish you would quit that," she stated more harshly than she had intended.

"Quit what?"

"Joking like that—"

"I'm not joking."

And one look at his grim-jawed determination quickly convinced her that he wasn't joking.

"Brant—" she began with a strangled sound.

He placed a strong hand in the air, stopping her speech as if he had power over her vocal cords. "Stop. I'll go a little easier. I have to keep reminding myself that although I've known for almost three years that I was going to marry you, this is new to you."

"Brant, I can never marry you!" Vickie gasped with dismay.

"There are no nevers, Vickie," he said calmly, smiling as he approached her and reached to raise her chin. "Now"—he spun her astonished, pliable form around and prodded her toward the bedroom—"go find something to set off that stunning figure and face. I'm taking you to meet a friend of mine, and I know he's going to be green with envy."

Vickie tried uselessly to mouth words, but none came to her lips. It was impossible to argue with Brant anyway; he ignored what he didn't want to hear and easily overrode his opponent.

109

When she reached her bedroom, she didn't have to think. Her femininity took over. Brant wanted to impress a friend, and she couldn't help but do her best to assist him, she told herself, swiftly searching her closet, looking for something light and casual but enticing.

A few minutes later she was critically evaluating her reflection. The dress was perfect. It was white, setting off the black sheen of her hair and the golden summer tan that covered her. The silk skirt flowed when she walked; both bodice and back were revealing but modest. A wide gold belt cinched her waistline, emphasizing its slenderness.

With a last stroke of a brush through her loose hair, Vickie closed a door in her mind. She could never marry Brant. The web of deception she had played would destroy them. But she had to be with him. She had to play this game to the end.

He was intensely engrossed in the morning paper when she emerged from her room, so engrossed that he didn't hear her light footfalls. Vickie moved behind his chair and placed a hand tentatively on his shoulder, shying away when he deftly caught it with his own without looking up. He smiled into the paper, then with amazing dexterity swung her around so that the paper disappeared and she gracefully fell to his lap simultaneously. Flushing, Vickie found herself chuckling at the pleased mischief in his eyes.

"I could have sworn you didn't hear me!" she murmured.

"I didn't," he agreed, the devilish leer of his eyes heart-stopping. "But I would have known that delicious scent a mile away."

Vickie was not surprised when his lips lowered over hers. She savored the sweet anticipation of their meeting. She circled willing arms around his neck, playing her fingers down its corded length, wallowing in the strength that held her, immersed in the flow of heat. Being loved by Brant was being dazzled by the sunlight and caressed by the moon all in one. The touch of his rough fingers was astoundingly earthy and sensual, yet it held the edge of starlit magic, a sheer physical magnetism that compelled her to another plane.

Her flesh was keenly sensitized to his, and she no longer attempted any form of denial. Her lips parted to his command; her tongue eagerly sought his. She could barely breathe as their embrace seemed to continue into eternity, nor did she care. As their mouths met in demanding exploration, they touched wildly, savoring each other's touch, and as Brant became newly familiar with the curves that boldly beckoned him through the soft touch of fabric, Vickie brought tenderly searching fingers over the rough tweed of his jacket, hypnotized by the feel and scent of him, and by the radiating energy of his being. She never felt so entirely alive as when she touched him, and felt his touch upon her. The flesh of her throat quavered as he lightly stroked it, as he held her, as the sensitive deep valley between her breasts where his moist kiss wandered shuddered, creating in its wake a tide that engulfed with molten fire.

She could refuse him nothing. Time and space had stood still to become a golden field of all-consuming, sensuous pleasure, pleasure heightened by the sweet anticipation of long-denied, greater joys to come. Floating, spinning, mindless, Vickie lost herself in the dual pounding of their hearts, in the weakening, dizzying gaspings that were her best effort at breathing.

Suddenly she found herself on her feet, set aside, as Brant rose beside her, startlingly angry. Quickly masking the hurt in her eyes, Vickie spun away from him, bewildered, straining for a sense of dignity.

"We'd better get going," was all that Brant had to say in way of explanation, his voice husky but curiously harsh.

They were in the car and halfway over the causeway before either of them spoke again, and surprisingly it was Vickie, her tone admirably impersonal and flatly clinical.

"I don't understand you, Brant. Supposedly you want me enough to marry me, and then when you can obviously have anything—"

He turned to her briefly with a frown, making an untouchable granite of his severe features. "You don't understand. I do want you, but I want you wanting me every bit as fervently—and consciously. Not just physically. Not just for the moment. I want you to know before I walk into a room that it's me that you want. I don't want you ever to think you came to me in an instant of madness—and it has nothing to do with marrying you. I want to marry you no matter what."

Harsh laughter bubbled in Vickie's throat, laughter that she bitterly contained. She had wanted Brant for three years, three years when despite all resolution she had been plagued by dreams that he would walk back into her life. These dreams had seemed impossible, had made all else impossible. But Vickie and Brant were on different wave lengths. Again, arguing was futile.

There was a hint of rain in the air, drawing a sharp but pleasing scent of salt from the bay. Cumulus clouds, puffed and magical, billowed high over the water, not yet containing the gray of the storm that would surely come by evening. The causeway was taking them out to the gulf islands, and Vickie forced herself to turn her mind to the immediate future.

"Where are we going?" she asked softly.

If Brant noticed her complete change of subject and tone, he gave no sign. His eyes following the expanse of the bridge were a frosty, unreadable blue.

"To the best Italian restaurant this side of Verona," he told her lightly. "Owned and operated by an old friend, fraternity brother, and Marine pal of mine. You should like him." Brant cast her a glance which was now amused. "He's one of your biggest fans."

"Mine!"

"Um. He sees every show at Monte's. He's sent me each interview with you in it for the last two years."

"I don't believe you!" Vickie charged, laughing, only to sober quickly at Brant's immediate reply: "I never lie."

Somewhat resentfully, she was sure he never did. Was there any safe avenue of conversation between them?

"What's your friend's name?" she inquired quickly.

"Frank, Frank Leonini. I spent as much time growing up in his house as I did in my own. You might say you're meeting part of the family."

He flashed her a dazzling smile, and suddenly Vickie relaxed.

112

He had just set the tone for the afternoon. There would be no questions, no pressure. It was just a date, a get-to-know-you date. And she was looking forward to the meal, her spirits soaring as high as the cumulus clouds.

A few moments later they drove down a mile of white beach, then abruptly turned down a pine trail. At its end, set high on a dune, was a rustic wooden structure with carved script declaring MAMA LEONINI'S.

The building was charming, secluded in the pine glen. Brant smiled at Vickie's obvious pleasure as he escorted her over a planked path that bridged a tiny stream alive with various vines and orchids and tropical fish. "Wait till you see where we're eating!" he advised her.

The interior, did, if anything, outshine the charming exterior. The food could be horrible, she decided, and people would still come to sit in this atmosphere.

A grotto had been created, a cavern of flowers, candles, breathtaking murals, and aromatic scents that titillated the nostrils. The setting was perfect for the plump lady with the dark hair and olive complexion who unabashedly descended upon them as soon as they entered, crying first, "Brant!" then spewing into rapid Italian that left Vickie with her head spinning just to listen.

Brant laughingly hugged the woman, begging, "Slow down, Mama! And meet Vickie."

With cheery and openly curious eyes, Mama Leonini turned to Vickie with a wide, encompassing smile. "I'm sorry, *figlio mio,* but you understand"—she reached on tiptoe to tousle Brant's hair as if he were a small, wayward child—"it has been so long! Vickie, is it? Welcome, welcome." With her warm brown eyes sparkling merrily away, she turned back to Brant. *"Che bella,* eh?"

"Yes," Brant chuckled, "Vickie is beautiful. Maybe I'd better not see Frankie!"

"Ach! My son!" Mama Leonini shook her head in lament and Vickie wasn't sure if it was Brant or Frankie she referred to. Vickie didn't have long to ponder the question. Mama Leonini slipped an arm conspiratorially through Vickie's and led her past the tables of scattered diners, whispering, "Both these boys of mine—tall, strong and rugged! But do I have a grandchild to show for it? No! Not even a daughter-in-law to love!"

"I'm trying to change that," Brant whispered from behind them. "But don't push, Mama, this one is skittish."

Vickie hadn't had a chance to utter a word, and she wasn't to get a chance for several minutes. She had been propelled out of the main dining room to an outdoor, covered terrace that over-looked the tranquil beach and a scattering of breeze-wafted palms. But like the main dining room, the terrace was as elegant as a Paris café on the Champs-Élysées. Tables and settings were in snowy white and bright red and candles flickered on the tables, not obliterated by the sun. And as Brant cordially seated Vickie in a plush velvet chair, she once more glanced up as a spew of Italian in a rich baritone vibrated into the clean air.

The voice had to be Frankie's. He was as tall and broad as Brant, suavely good-looking, and as dark as Brant was light. As his mother had, he embraced Brant with no hesitation, then turned swiftly to Vickie, his dark eyes appreciative of her.

"Victoria!" he breathed, and his voice was a caress. He took her hand with tender gallantry. "Once again Brant wins out!" His statement was given with no rancor, yet it was endearingly sincere.

"You must be Frankie," Vickie smiled, unable to do anything but enjoy the camaraderie of those around her. It was a family, a close-knit family, and she had been decreed a part of it.

"Yes, a heartbroken Frankie, I'm afraid!" he told her.

"Cut the dramatics," Brant interposed with a false severity. "I'm supposed to be the actor, you know."

"Hey, what dramatics?" Frankie complained, drawing his mother a chair and seating himself. With dark, enchanted eyes for Vickie only, he continued. "The girl of my dreams—and the blond hero here tells me he's marrying her!"

Vickie opened her mouth to object, then let it fall shut. She wasn't up to discrediting Brant in front of these marvelously enthusiastic people. Maybe it was more than that. She wanted

114

to live the dream she had harbored so long. But it couldn't last. Like a moth she was flitting ever closer to the flame, and she seemed to have no control.

And it really didn't matter. Before she could collect her scattered thoughts, the conversation had moved on. Wine and cheese and fruit appeared on the table, served unobtrusively by black-jacketed waiters with pleasant white grins. Vickie had never been more thoroughly entertained. Although the talk was general, she learned more about Brant in that half hour than she could have anywhere else in a week. Frankie was full of stories, and he had a gift for telling them. She could well imagine the two of them as very young men, hell-raising their way through college, sobering in the jungles of Vietnam, floundering as they sought out careers.

"An actor!" Frankie proclaimed, shaking his head with disbelief. "And I laughed! I told Brant to stick with something that was dress shirts and ties!"

"I surely never imagined a restaurateur with the finest wine cellar in the South," Brant retorted. "Damn! There was a time when this man didn't know Chablis from Burgundy!"

"Eh! Enough, you two!" Mama Leonini chastised them both affectionately. "Frankie, come on. We have work in the kitchen."

"No, we don't," Frankie protested with a guileless grin.

"Yes, you do!" Brant taunted. "The pasta maker called in sick."

Grimacing, Frankie rose. "Okay, blond hero, get on to the romantic session of your lunch. But don't forget to eat, eh? We've planned everything around you for the day!"

The warmth created by the familiar pair remained when mother and son left, yet Vickie was suddenly swept by inhibition. Watching the candle rather than Brant's face, she murmured, "Your friends are very nice."

"Too nice!" Brant grinned, slipping a hand over hers. "I'm going to have to watch out for Frankie, I can see."

"Why don't we just fix him up with Terry?" Vickie asked mischievously.

115

"That's not a bad idea," Brant agreed. "Save us both those little itches of jealousy!"

Their lunch began to arrive in a stream of platters that seemed endless. They were served soup, antipasto, and salad, and then a variety of pastas. Moaning that she couldn't take another bite, Vickie was dismayed to find they hadn't been served the main course yet. Certain she would never fit into her costume later that night, Vickie still managed to do justice to the tray of tender veal and peppers that appeared next. Dessert, however, was out of the question.

"Just cappuccino," Brant assured her. "The best you'll have in the States, I guarantee you."

They settled on the cappuccino. The wine, the meal, the easy-going company, all had left Vickie in an amazingly indolent state, comfortable and lulled off-guard. Lazed back in the cushion of her chair, with the tranquility of the breeze and sea before her, Vickie was astounded by Brant's sudden question.

"Why the Langley, Vickie?"

"What?" Her eyes snapped to his, the mask of coolness reaching them too late.

"You heard me," he said grimly. "And don't hedge around, telling me that you don't know what I'm talking about."

"Langley is my name," Vickie said, facing him but blinking rapidly as she desperately wondered just what he did mean.

"A stage name?"

"It's just my name," she retorted.

"Your name?" Brant persisted, not touching her but commanding her attention with the tone of his voice. "There never was a Mr. Langley, was there?"

"Really, Brant," Vickie began indignantly, her spine stiffening with the panic that raced beneath the surface of her rigid composure. "My past is none of your business, and I'll thank you to remember that."

"Your past *is* my business, because I'm your future. Being honest with me is going to cut out a few of the ridiculous problems between us. And it's stupid as hell for you to keep lying, because I know you're lying. There never was a Mr. Langley."

Looking into his eyes, Vickie desperately stalled for time. He returned her stare with the opaqueness of a stormcloud. What did he know? a voice screamed to her inside her head. Not about Mark. He couldn't. He wasn't condemning her; he was simply demanding an answer.

"No," she said coolly, picking up her demitasse cup. "There was never a Mr. Langley. I picked the name out of the phone book."

"That was imaginative," Brant said dryly. "Why all the lies?"

"Why?" Vickie was surprised she didn't shout the word. What an incredible question. *Why?* "Because," she stuttered. "Oh, Brant! That's completely obvious!"

He shrugged, and his magnificent shoulders hunched toward her as the opaque quality left his eyes to be replaced by a tender compassion.

"Obvious to you, maybe, but silly. You're afraid of what would have been said. Or of vicious tongues."

"You're not big on vicious tongues yourself?" Vickie reminded him curtly. "You had a fit over those interviews."

"Only because they had been given by someone I trusted."

"I see," she told him icily. "Well, I don't really trust anyone. And I'd definitely appreciate it if you would consider what I've told you as a confidence."

He tossed back his head and his laughter rang into the salt air. "Christ, Vickie, I'm not after information for anyone else! *I* want to understand you! I had to know what was making you tick—what was making you so afraid. Terrified of the word *marriage.*"

"Brant, you're a fool!" Vickie charged him, staring out over the ocean. "I still can't marry you. We live in different worlds. I'd be terrified of marriage to you because I want a marriage that means forever, and you come from a place where it means until we grow tired of each other."

"Stop it, Victoria!" The sound of Brant's voice grated harshly in her ear. "I come from Tampa. And marriage means the same thing to me as it does to you. Yes, we'll have career problems. We'll have lots of things to work out. But so does every couple.

They make a commitment—one of love. And that means compromise and working the problems out together."

The irresistible urge to cry was seeping through Vickie. She kept her gray gaze out to sea and fought the tears that were slowly encroaching, like the incoming tide. A scratched recording echoed again and again through her mind—Brant's matter-of-fact statement that he never lied.

"I don't know, Brant, I just don't know," she murmured.

"I won't pressure you," he promised, adding with a teasing voice that didn't reassure her when he added, "I intend to give you at least two weeks. Now, what about Mark?"

"What about him?" Vickie gasped, feeling a world of darkness closing in around her.

"What about his father? Will I be able to adopt him?"

"Brant, please, you're going way too fast! I, uh, I don't know what I feel for you, I don't know—"

"I know," he interrupted dismissively. "I'm planning ahead. What about Mark's father?"

"He's dead."

"He really is?" Brant's words were not a question to her, but a musing to himself. "One day, Vickie, you're going to tell me all about it. You were hurt badly, that's obvious, and I want to share all those hurts with you. I want to bring them out in the open, air them, and let them fade."

Vickie's most terrible urge was to laugh, not with amusement, but with dry, bitter agony. The more he offered, the more evident his sincerity became, the worse she felt. He was handing her the moon, but her fingers were too slippery to take it. Opportunities to bare the truth and her soul were coming to her on silver platters, and she watched them all drift by, shocked by the lies she automatically told. She should have told him when he asked, but without conscious thought she had spoken the words she had ingrained into her mind. And now the moment when she could have told the truth was gone, lost in the gray web of deception she seemed powerless to break.

"I don't know, Brant," she heard herself saying again. "This is all too sudden. . . . I need time."

"We have time," he promised her, taking her fingers with a gentleness that seemed impossible for such powerful hands. He kissed each one, watching her eyes, moving his mouth with inherent sensuality over each, drawing a shiver from her as his teeth grazed the last one.

He stood suddenly, and his voice was rich and husky. "We've got to get back; you have to pack and you have a show to do tonight."

Trancelike, Vickie rose with him.

The sky was changing as they bade fond farewell to the Leoninis and walked down the planked path to the car. Pink streaks tapering to crimson threads wove their way beneath a sun now shadowed by clouds turned gray. The weather touched Vickie's heart as an omen. Nothing could ever be simple and clear again. But then, despite all shields drawn, nothing had been clear for almost three years. It had just taken her until now to realize it.

CHAPTER SIX

As was usual, the show went off without a hitch. A tribute to willpower, Vickie decided. No matter what went on in the mind, it was possible to make the body function normally. She could talk, walk, and breathe and appear to be tranquil. If one acted tranquilly and serenely at ease long enough, one became so. It wasn't really anything new. Three years ago she had forged a wall of resignation, and therefore tranquility. She had moved through life with a pleasant dignity because of that. Suddenly it seemed possible again. The answers had been within her reach all the time. Now she had to be sure Brant was serious. She would never be completely free of fear knowing Brant's temper as she did. But the lie she retained and the admission forced out of her began to jell to her advantage. Brant knew she had never been married, yet he still bore no suspicions regarding Mark.

It was actually perfect. She loved Brant; one day she would have to tell him about Mark. Explain everything that she had felt, everything that she had done. But how much better to tell him if they could build a life together! Their life would begin with deceit, but surely not a terrible one. Brant was already fond of Mark; presumably he would be thrilled to discover, eventually, that his adoptive son was his own.

Vickie could even admit the truth and assure Edward with a clear conscience that she would indeed tell Brant one day. He would understand. There was more to her decision to hold back than just the uneasy fear of reaction. She couldn't tell Brant now for the same reason she didn't three years ago. He might begin insisting on marriage for the sake of the child, an arrangement that was sure to be a disaster.

She had lived too long and gone through too much to settle for anything less in marriage than the total bond of a one-to-one commitment she had always dreamed of. A till-death-do-us-part commitment based on love.

Her dream was becoming a reachable star, as long as Brant was serious, and not living out summer fantasies of long ago.

Tonight she didn't care. Scrubbing her face clean of stage makeup and applying just a glimmer of lipstick and a swift wand of mascara, Vickie grew recklessly exuberant. She was taking a chance, but she dryly assured herself that all life was a chance. She was gambling the high wall of safety it had taken long to build, but the possible rewards defied her dreams and imagination.

"You seem disgustingly cheerful," Terry told her idly, breaking her inner concentration. The brunette perched languidly against the dressing table. "Did you decide to go up to the panhandle tomorrow?"

"Umm. I'll be there," Vickie replied evasively.

"How nice," Terry said, but catching her gaze in the mirror, Vickie was sure Terry considered her proposed presence as anything but nice. Apparently Terry was still carrying her own torch for Brant.

Unable to forget the trouble Terry was capable of causing and still not sure of Brant's immunity, Vickie smiled sweetly. "I'm sure it will be a very nice little vacation. Excuse me, will you." Still holding her smile bright, she swept around Terry. Later the brunette would discover she had left with Brant, and she could fume all she liked.

Chuckling slightly as she entered the empty hallway, Vickie chastised herself for the smug and, yes, malicious, satisfaction she was feeling. But she was only human, and Terry was a born troublemaker as well as a born beauty. Supposed bonds of friendship were as fragile as silk if they stood in her way.

Her smile was still delicately curved into her lips as she reached the parking lot and sought out Brant. He was so easy to find, a silhouette as tall and sturdy as an oak in the darkness, his hair a golden beam of guiding light as he lounged against the Mercedes, waiting. For her. His eyes, following her from the indolent shade of thick honey lashes, welcomed her with devilish appreciation, their blue as warm as a summer's day. With her new reckless take-a-chance mood, Vickie walked straight to him, stood on tiptoe, and brushed his lips with a feather-light kiss of promise.

"Ummm . . ." he murmured, cocking a speculative brow as she lowered to her heels, still smiling enigmatically. "To what do I owe this magnificent change of heart?"

"Never a change of heart," Vickie told him in a grave whisper, her tone wistful. "I think you collected my heart with a string of others on the day I first saw you."

Her abrupt change to candor was stunning to Brant, but he forced himself to usher her calmly into the car without saying a word. He wanted to tread carefully and not tamper with the return of a love he once discovered and nurtured too late.

But something had changed. Vickie was relaxed. And she was more stunning than ever. Her hair spilled over her shoulders in endless black waves that were streaked with a gloss of blue—a night ocean, alive beneath the moon. The thin veil of frost was gone from her gray eyes that met his clearly with the starlit eternity of deepest space. And she warmed to his touch without the slightest flinch.

Brant eased the car out of the parking lot and drove silently until they had left the city limits of Sarasota behind and came upon the coastal road. Then he glanced across the car at Vickie. "If I have your heart," he told her wickedly, "how about scooting over here and lending me a shoulder?"

Vickie complied, wondering for just a moment if she had given too much away. No, her statement had been a teasing one, easily said. Brant Wicker knew he collected hearts on a string and tonight was a date, an exploration, nothing more. More would be in the future. But her guard was down; she was a healthy, normal, mature young woman out with a man she loved. But she was older now, savvy, careful, and totally aware of the conse-

122

quences. And also totally receptive to the strong arm that rested behind her shoulder, she told herself dryly.

Fearing that she had taken a step further than she intended, Vickie began to make light conversation, discussing anything that came to her mind. But despite her efforts, each line of dialogue turned to something deeper. A clinical conversation on the pros and cons of living in New York City led her to silently wonder if she could find work in New York if Brant returned to Broadway. Could she be a success with such tremendous competition? Could two careers be harmonious? Would he expect her to give hers up? No, it wasn't going to be New York. Not right away. Brant had mentioned doing a movie.

Somewhere along the line the incredible happened. Despite the whirling tempest of her mind, Vickie fell asleep on Brant's shoulder. She awoke with a start to find the night still black and the hum of the car quiet. She hastily shifted her head to look up, and found Brant silently watching her, his features a stern mask of austerity in the green illumination of the dash.

"We're here," he said softly.

"This is it?" Vickie inquired, struggling from the lassitude of sleep and experiencing a moment of self-incrimination. Step right up, said the spider to the fly. And the fly was in the web of its own accord.

"This is it," Brant replied, his voice edged with amusement.

"Well," Vickie said briskly, sliding to let herself out of the car. "Let's see this palace of Monte's."

"Ah, yes, Monte's pleasure palace," Brant mused behind her, deliberately sinister. "By all means, let's view it quickly."

Feeling none too confident with his breath at her back, Vickie threw off a careless shrug and hurried up the hedged tile path to the redwood building that awaited them. Even in the pale light of moon and stars she could see that the "cottage" was exquisite. It rose from sand and dunes in a split-level, eye-pleasing symmetry, like an oasis in the desert.

"Would you like the key?" Brant inquired politely as she paused blankly at the door.

123

"Thanks," Vickie replied wryly, standing back for him to open it and turn on the lamps.

They both paused in the entryway. To the left, stairs wound majestically to a balcony that overlooked the fur-carpeted living room and offered a view of numerous doors—presumably the bedrooms. At the rear of the living room to the right, taking the entire back wall, were sliding doors of glass, giving a view of the Gulf that was breathtaking. The palms lining the beach were scarcely moving, nor did the water appear to be more than benevolent—sheer, shimmering glass like the doors that framed it.

"Monte does have taste!" Vickie murmured, teetering on the brink of a cold sweat of fear despite the humidity. Nonsense, she told herself, taking a breath to saunter up the inviting staircase. They were two adults; she had made no commitments as yet. Except in her own mind. Brant would force nothing from her.

Arguments raced on in her mind so loudly that she barely heard Brant's answer. "Yes, the man has taste."

"I'm going to pick out a room for myself," Vickie called gaily, leaning over the balcony.

Brant tilted his chin to look up at her, his eyes narrow slits of mirthful blue fire. "You do that, Juliet," he teased. "Or is it Rapunzel?" he asked as her raven hair floated over the carved bannister. Saluting her with a deviltry that assured her he was reading her mind, Brant backed toward the front door. "I'll go get the luggage."

Vickie meandered through the various bedrooms, averting her eyes from the beds. The beachhouse was furnished in the most elegant of contemporary styles. Chrome, glass, and shag carpeting were everywhere, as was wicker and thick, inviting cushions.

Vickie decided on the last room she entered, one facing the beach, and painted a light, sunshine yellow, complemented by earth tones in the decor. Moving to the high, draped window, she could see the water in the glow of the moon. Without realizing it, she curled her hands around the cloth of the rust-colored drapes.

124

"What is this, *Cat on a Hot Tin Roof?*" Brant inquired from the doorway.

Self-consciously, Vickie dropped the drapes. "Did you find something you like?" she asked coolly.

"Umm," he replied with an assured grin that made her want to slap him. "Right next door." He set her suitcase on the foot of the bed. "Have you got a bathing suit in this thing?"

"Of course."

"Good, get it on."

"Now? It must be at least three A.M.!"

"Actually," Brant said, leaving her with the grinning arrogance that his order would be obeyed, "it's closer to four."

"You're crazy!" Vickie called after him. "I'm not going swimming now!"

The bedroom door, which had been closing, reopened, and Brant's blond head reappeared. "Sure you are!" he said nicely. His grin hardened a fraction. "With or without a suit. See you in a minute."

Luckily the door shut before her mouth fell open. She had heard Brant speak with that sword-edged civility before. It meant he was determined to have his way, and to take any steps to achieve it.

Prudence overrode her instinct to tell him she simply wasn't going swimming; he was welcome to be shark bait himself if he wished. The picture of Brant dressing her in her brief bikini was less than dignified. The imagining was so undignified that she was changed in less than the allotted minute and waited on the balcony with a white terry robe tied over her bathing suit.

Brant emerged from his door just seconds after she, clad only in cutoffs, a towel slung carelessly around his neck. He showed no sign of surprise at Vickie's quick appearance, and as his eyes swept over her in a fraction of a second, she found herself returning the gesture and admitting to herself as her eyes took him in that he was a superb specimen of humanity. There wasn't a spare inch of flesh on his body; his every movement was a play of perfectly toned muscle. He was a performer, she told herself. His body was his tool. Like any instrument, it had to be cared for.

125

"Shall we raid the refrigerator first?" Brant suggested.

Vickie quirked an eloquent brow. "Is there going to be something in it to raid?"

"Oh, I assume," Brant murmured, fixing a hand on the small of her back to lead her down the stairs. "I'm willing to bet on a fruity, impeccably dry white wine and a fine assortment of cheeses. Perhaps some apples. A little forbidden fruit always comes in handy."

The refrigerator contained much more than the items Brant had mentioned. It was stocked to serve an army.

"How did Monte manage all this?" Vickie mused, accepting the bottle of wine and crystal glasses Brant forced into her hands. Brant didn't answer. He kept his head stuck in the refrigerator, searching for a Saran-wrapped tray.

"Monte didn't manage all this!" Vickie charged with crisp harshness as suspicion became as clear as glass. "You did!"

The refrigerator clicked shut. "Guilty." Brant stared at her with no trace of apology.

"And this house?" she asked icily.

He shrugged. "Mine."

"This is a rather elaborate set-up."

"Yes."

"I think I will go swimming," Vickie said coldly. "By myself, thank you."

Clinking the wine and glasses down on the Formica counter with such vehemence that the crystal threatened to shatter, Vickie sailed out of the kitchen and stumbled to the back doors. So much for serious relationships! He had wanted her all right, and everything said and done from that point had all been part of a plot. She might have found the entire scenario amusing, and might have even ignored it and laughed it off, had the man been anyone but Brant.

He caught her just as she fumbled with the rather complicated lock on the sliding doors. As if a wind had swept by her, she found herself twirling around, feeling no pain, but turned with the force of a tornado.

"What the hell is this all about?" Brant demanded angrily. His

126

back rested against the glass, his arms crossed over his chest. She could see the coarse curls on his chest rise and fall with the play of taut muscles as he breathed.

"I don't appreciate being played for a fool," Vickie grated, digging her nails into the palms of her hand to stand before him without flinching, her chin thrust to a regal elevation.

"What?" He shook his head in disbelief.

"All the plotting and planning—"

"So what?"

"So what?" Vickie repeated, shaking her head. Her mouth opened, but she couldn't seem to form words for an explanation. "Just let me out, will you please, Brant. I'd like to be alone."

"No. I'd like to hear what this latest problem of yours is."

She knew damned well he wasn't going to budge. His eyes had never been icier, the line of his full lips more grim or tight. But she didn't want him near her, touching her, right now. It was too easy to accept his brand of lies.

"I told you when you came back to the theater to go after Terry," she said, her voice containing a slight wince. If he touched Terry, she would go crazy, implode.

"Hell," Brant muttered disgustedly, his bewildered anger making his words harsh and cold as a stone wall. "At least Terry occasionally makes sense."

"I'm making sense, and you know it!"

"The hell I do!" he yelled. His fists clenched over his folded arms and Vickie was sure he controlled an urge to shake her.

Back down, she warned herself. Lowering her lashes, she murmured, "I can't make any one-sentence explanations." Trying to appear sheepish while still shaking at some inner core with hurt and an anger of her own, she added softly, "Get the wine and we'll talk."

If she had been thinking rationally, she would have realized an attempt to dupe Brant was the least intelligent thing she could do. Nor was she thinking that even if she succeeded in eluding him, she would be in trouble for hours to come. But she had lost all cool, rational thought. Her normal, controlled thinking processes had been absent since Brant returned.

127

Nor did she give a damn about the hours to come. All she wanted was to find a berth of safety away from him, a place where she wasn't reduced to longing by the sight of him, tremors from the anger she had elicited. Withdrawal wasn't defeat.

. . .

As soon as Brant grudgingly eyed her with a cynical warning and strode out of sight in the hallway, Vickie found the pin in the door's lock and bolted it. She ran ridiculously down the beach with no place to go, the salt and sand and gentle surf a padding for her bare feet.

It was pathetic, the soft thud of her footsteps pounding in her ears. Where was Victoria, the woman who could handle anything with the blink of a commanding gray eye? The woman who thought and spoke, and never behaved on wild impulse?

She didn't hear him coming. He was as fleet and silent as a rabbit on the sand. One second she was running, the next she was spinning. And then she was on the ground, the wind knocked cleanly from her lungs, the force of her fall shielded by Brant's body. A superb tackle. Hindsight told her she should have expected no less.

He shifted and she was locked beneath him on the sand, staring into enigmatic pools of deep-set blue ice, fighting for breath to rail against him. She found some satisfaction in seeing that he was as winded as she; it had taken him a bit of effort to catch up.

She tried to speak, but instead of finding words, her lower lip trembled as her mouth parted. The pink tip of her tongue edged out to moisten the dryness that had parched her lips. Then everything she had been wanting to say left her mind as well as her tongue. The blue of his eyes began to mist before her as Brant lowered his head over hers and took her lips with a gentle, poignant yearning that belied any anger. He tasted of the wine; his scent was that of the surrounding sea. To resist him would be like trying to hold back the flooding tides of the ocean.

His tongue explored every succulent recess of her mouth. Then his kisses became butterflies that fluttered over her face, her cheeks, her eyelids, light as a breeze. But they wouldn't end

128

there. Despite the soft enticement of his sensuously teasing mouth, the arms that held her were vibrantly alive with heat and passion; his entire, sinewed being was taut.

With a shivered groan Brant encapsulated her head with his hands, raking his fingers through the raven hair that spewed across the sand like a silk covering, and brought his hovering chest to rest next to hers. His face was buried in her neck as he murmured, "Let me lie down beside you, babe . . ."

Vickie's fingers moved to his head, sinking into his hair. It was the only gold she would ever covet. Her hands moved downward then, over his back, trembling as they ran down the strength of his spine. Her eyes were closed, clenched tight, but she could see him with her hands, trace the beloved pattern of his body. On the taut muscle of his left shoulder blade there was a tiny scar; above that was a smattering of faint freckles, made darker by the sun. And as her fingers played lower, over a bronzed expanse of ribs, they found a tiny mole just above his left hip.

His cheek moved against hers, slightly and deliciously rough with the dawning of an early morning beard. His tongue invaded her ear, drawing moist lazy circles that tensed her fingers immediately, and she clung to him, still at a loss of words, wondering vaguely if she cared to find any or not. The breeze that wafted over them was cooled by the water. She shivered. But she wasn't cold. Brant's heat was encasing her, infusing her, lapping her with a flame that entered the deepest center of her desire with a soaring blue flame. Vickie twisted to kiss the hollow of his neck, moving the tip of her tongue erotically, grazing him with small nibbles.

The result was an earthquake, an eruption of need, and a groan that threatened to split the ground asunder. She was immersed in his embrace, rolling with him along the sand, shedding her robe in the process. His hands steamed over her body like molten lava, sensitizing her flesh for the moist fire of the lips that followed in their path. He didn't touch her skimpy suit at first, but aroused her to levels of insanity by making love through the sheer knit, making her feverishly toss and writhe beneath him as his fingers and then his mouth taunted her nipples to rigid peaks that strained against the fabric.

Only then did he release the ties of her bra top, to continue his torture with ever enlarging circles of his tongue that became figure-eights over her breasts. Both roseate peaks were then assaulted afresh with a fervent suckling that created a mindless whirlpool of pleasure, only to be deserted as his kisses followed his hands to strip her of the bikini bottom.

Vickie was fire herself, unable to keep still. His cutoffs did nothing to hide his desire, and they were a poor shield between them. The core of her being, demanding only satiation, went with her fingers as they moved to his snap. There was no hesitation to the hands that brought down his zipper with an ardent rasp. The cutoffs were gone. Brant was beautifully beside her, his masculinity throbbing its yearning to possess her. He was a golden god sent from the heavens. She found her voice.

"Oh, Brant . . ."

His thoughts weren't much different as he gazed at her with the passion and awe of ageless centuries. She was all things to him, a Guinevere to be adored on a pedestal, a wild, passionate, raven-haired wood-nymph, a sweet, honeyed rose, a seductress, a temptress, an arrogant Morgan le Fay. His woman. All that woman should be . . . She was exquisite, her skin creamy against the sand, her waist his handspan, the intoxicating mounds of her breasts perfect for his devouring lips. Her hips fit to his with an unbelievable, harmonious rhythm. The enchanting gray eyes that returned his stare with no restraint were as deep as the earth, loving and trusting and incredibly sultry. . . .

He had a simple answer for her. "I love you, Victoria."

And then he was tumultuously inside her, their coupling the magical combination of the intensity of love and the fulfillment of long-awaited and dreamed of desire. Each aching thrust of elegant madness drove Vickie deeper into the abyss of culminating sensation, arching and writhing for every touch of fevered delight.

"Brant!"

His name was an explosive whisper of ecstasy. Her eyes flew open to absorb the elation that did not end with the shattering of their passion, but flooded through her with a tender change of character. Brant did not leave her, but held her tenderly as they both shuddered beneath the stars that had seemed to multiply dizzyingly in the sky. Gradually sounds became coherent again, the soft pounding of the surf, the barely discernible rustle of the breeze through the palms. Her body was so sensitized that she felt each grain of sand in their earthen bed as well as each breath Brant took, every twitch of a muscle.

"I love you," he told her again, raising himself just high enough to see her eyes. "Forever."

With wonder, she lifted a hand to smooth back the ever-straying tendril of hair that fell over his eye. "I love you," she admitted, "it's all so hard to believe. . . ."

"What," he challenged gently, "that I love you, or that you love me?"

"Oh, Brant," Vickie murmured, wrapping her arms back around his neck and pulling him down so that she could bury her head in his shoulder. "You're adored all the time!" she mumbled brokenly. "I've been so afraid . . ."

"Adored, Vickie, not really loved. Not for myself, for the man that I am. Love is a very special thing, between very special people only. There are a million shallow counterparts, but the real thing is rare and precious."

Was the salt on her cheek a taste of tears, or a mist of the sea? she wondered. "Brant, I'm so sorry," she whispered. "I thought, I thought . . ."

"You thought I was rigging a simple seduction," he answered for her, his hands soothing as they created soft patterns over her ribs that seemed a subtle extension of the air. "Well, it was all rigged, but not the way you thought. I was willing to go to any end to be with you. I knew you were free, but I also saw you were prickly as a pear near me. I knew you didn't trust me; I had to take every opportunity to prove myself."

"Then you really want to marry me?" Vickie murmured, a

little awed. "Brant, we could never make it."

"Why not?"

"You are Brant Wicker."

"Yes, I am," he agreed, shifting to an elbow to better observe her as she lay in the sand, a naked sea nymph, an exquisite daughter of Neptune with eyes that portrayed the depths of the oceans, the gray tranquility, the tormented storms that could rage.

"A star in the heavens is beautiful," Vickie purred, touching his sandy shoulder, unable as he to draw away. "But it can't be captured. . . ."

"Damn, you do need a swim!" Brant was suddenly on his feet with her in his arms, walking slowly to the surf. "I am not," he said sternly, "a star in the heavens. I'm a man—one who loves you completely, who wants to spend his life with you."

Glancing at him adoringly as they moved into the tepid water, Vickie said, "But I'm afraid I'm a very jealous woman where you're concerned. All those other leading ladies . . ."

"We'll work together as much as possible," Brant said with a shrug. "I admit to a fairly jealous nature myself. We'll seek each other's approval before commiting to any project."

"But Brant—"

"But you do need a swim!" he countered. "Something to clear those 'buts' out of that webbed brain of yours!"

He released her and she sank into the surf, only to be recaptured.

"But what?" he demanded gruffly.

"Oh, there are still a million buts!" Vickie answered, laughing as she wiped the salt water from her face, not the least of which was Mark. But she couldn't worry about that now. She knew what she was doing. The time would come.

"But," Vickie insisted, winding her arms around his slick wet neck and pressing close to his flesh, relishing the sensation. "I can't think of anything more right at the minute. Except that I don't even know which coastline you're actually living on and I have a permanent job in Sarasota."

"I liked it better when you weren't thinking!" Brant scowled. "Maybe you need another swim!"

She was back in the water again, and this time she did swim. Together they followed the shoreline, their bodies close, radiating warmth through the water. Eventually they tired of their play and returned to the sand to collect their clothing.

"I hope you haven't any close neighbors." Vickie shivered as Brant leisurely dried her, titillating her skin afresh.

Regretfully, he wraped her terry robe back around her. "If I do," he said with a lascivious smile, "let's hope they're not into voyeurism!"

"Brant!"

"Come on. Let's head back to the house and nibble on some cheese and indulge in that wine I was tasting before you decided on a disappearing act!"

Hand in hand they returned to the house. "I think we should take the tray upstairs," Brant suggested, his eyes narrowed. "I want to clarify several of those buts for you, and you seem to comprehend things so much better in a reclining position!"

"Seduce me and I'll agree to anything?" Vickie inquired dryly.

"Something like that."

"You're terrible!"

"Really?" He came close and nuzzled her ear while sneaking a hand beneath her robe and along her thigh, inching it ever higher. "I thought I was rather good. . . ."

"Incorrigible!" Vickie corrected herself, spinning from his touch. "Maybe I'd better take the tray."

The pink light of dawn was streaking through the window as they entered Brant's room, arrayed in a gentle prism of early morning colors. Vickie snatched a piece of cheese and gnawed it as she stood before the window, wondering if a day would ever dawn so beautifully again.

Brant came behind her, enveloping her with his arms as he handed her a glass of wine. "To Mrs. Brant Wicker," he murmured.

Vickie turned in his arms so quickly that she spilled wine on

133

them both, exclaiming, "What a mess! Salt water and wine—".

"I'll cherish each taste," Brant promised, kissing her collarbone with lips that seemed insatiable.

"I need a shower—"

"Not now, woman!" He took her hand and demurely adjusted her robe before leading her to sit on the bed. "Talk about plotting," he told her ruefully, "I really do have this well plotted out. We're getting married next week. Then we have a summer of *Othello* here. Then how do you feel about a movie?"

Vickie carefully bit into another piece of cheese and sipped her wine before answering. "I know you're doing the movie, Brant, and that's why I think we should wait."

He emitted a long groan of exasperation. "Not me, Vickie, you."

Her eyes hit his directly. "What do you mean?"

He chewed a piece of cheese long and carefully, his eyes sparkling with devilment. "There just happens to be a part in this film for a sexy Russian spy."

"Oh?" She busied herself with spreading a cracker with a glob of Camembert. "What makes you think the casting director would find me, with no film experience, right for this Russian spy?"

"The casting director has seen you," Brant said blandly, digging into the Camembert himself.

"Damn it!" Vickie lost all patience and snatched his cracker from him. "What are you saying?"

"Hey!" Brant growled, snatching his cracker back and gently moving the tray as he leaped over her and pinioned her to the bed. "I'm a contemporary man," he stated sternly, munching as he held her with one hand, "and I'll be proud to allow my brilliant wife a career, but," he growled fiercely, heedless of the giggles he was receiving, "I'll be damned if that same wife is going to give me fits in the bedroom."

"Brant!" Vickie wailed beseechingly.

"All right, sweetheart, I'll give it to you straight and simple." He did a wonderful Bogart imitation. "I had the casting director in the audience of *Godspell* the other night. Clancy thinks you'll be perfect."

"I don't believe you!"

"Well, it's true, I told you I never lie."

A shiver swept through Vickie, an icy wind that permeated her limbs. It felt like the old adage of someone stepping on her grave. A foreboding of disaster . . .

It was amazing that Brant couldn't feel the terrible cold. But he didn't. He kept on talking. "Besides," he told her with a broad grin, "I own the production company doing the film."

"I might be horrible!" Vickie warned him, part of her automatically responding to his words, another part of her still in a distant land of worry. Now was the time to tell him.

"You won't be," he said simply. "And now that all the buts are taken care of—"

"Can it really be that simple?" Vickie said softly, meaning far more than he knew.

"Love is simple," Brant told her, "if we let it be."

"Oh, God, Brant," Vickie shuddered violently, drawing herself as closely as possible to him with a feverish intensity. "I do love you, but I'm still afraid. . . ."

"Not with me, my love. I want to spend my life with you, and chauvinistically protect you all my days."

He made love to her again with an agonizing expertise, escalating them both to a wild and erotic abandon with hands that teased and demanded and burning wet kisses that delved into every secret of her womanhood. And as his heat diminished any thought of cold, Vickie returned his touch, all hesitancy lost in the desire to give the ardent, spiraling pleasure she received. As a lover, as a man, he was part angel, part devil. The delight he drove her to was as tempestuous as hell, as exalted as heavenly bliss.

Only as she lay still beside him again, held in his arms, her legs tangled with his, his even breathing telling her that he slept in perfect contentment, and the pink dawn had turned to full yellow light, did she find the time to worry again. But nothing, she knew, would allow her to chance an immediate end to the soaring, unbelievable happiness in her heart. The deception would have to go on until the timing was right to admit the truth.

She was right; she had to be right. Nothing else could influence his decision. Not the child she adored, not the past. Within a lifetime together, the right moment would come.

If she were so right, she wondered, why did the doubts continue to plague her, keeping her awake long after Brant slept?

CHAPTER SEVEN

"I've found them!"

The long, laconic drawl brought Vickie back from a deep sleep. Blinking rapidly to acclimate herself to the bright light of midday, and to the fact that someone was unabashedly standing in the doorway, Vickie instinctively grabbed the covers. A movement beside her warned her that Brant was also groggily awakening.

"My, my, aren't they as cute as two peas in a pod!"

Thought processes hit Vickie before her eyes focused. It was Terry. It had to be. She was the only person Vickie knew with the audacity to stare at someone in bed. And then make herself look merely concerned.

"Terry," Brant murmured, shaking his head slightly as if he didn't quite believe his eyes. "What are you doing here?"

"I was invited," Terry laughed brittlely. "We've all been looking for you. We saw the car but couldn't find you anywhere!"

"Well," Brant said dryly. "Here we are." He could feel Vickie tensing beside him, and his annoyance with Terry increased. The encounter didn't bother him, but he knew Vickie was disturbed. She could come to him without inhibitions, but her moral fiber shied from any form of public exhibition. He was surprised she hadn't crawled all the way beneath the sheets yet.

But she didn't move. He could almost feel her stiffening her shoulders before she smiled glacially and said, "Terry, do you mind . . ."

Whether Terry minded or not was never to be learned. Bobby appeared behind her and nodded briefly to the couple in the bed

137

before taking Terry's arm forcefully and pulling her from the bedroom. The door was shut sharply by Bobby's hand, and his words echoed to them, "Damnation, Terry, you've got the morals of an alley cat. . . ."

Brant peered quickly at Vickie to see the effect of the unannounced visit upon her. But her eyes met his with amusement and together they broke into laughter.

"Bobby always has had a way with Terry," Vickie commented, snuggling more closely to Brant beneath the sheets.

"Do you mind?"

"Do I mind?"

"Welllll," Brant admitted roughly, "if I had thought you were interested in anyone, I would have assumed that anyone to be Bobby."

"Oh, I am interested in Bobby," Vickie taunted with wide, wicked eyes. "He's a very good friend."

"How good?"

"Good."

"Clarify that, woman!" Brant demanded, grabbing her beneath the sheets in a swift movement that caught her deftly beneath his weight. He was teasing, but also intent on an answer.

"Like a brother," Vickie said demurely, her vow sincere.

"Well, that's good," Brant chuckled. "I rather like him myself, and I'd just as soon not be worried about you and him." He scowled darkly in an abrupt change of mood. "Is there anyone I should be worrying about?"

Tenderly stroking the angular planes of the face sternly staring down at her, Vickie smiled. "No one. I haven't been near anyone since—" She broke off her own words with horror. Brant followed her train of thought, but, luckily, still in the wrong direction.

"Since Mark's father?" he finished for her, his hardened expression fathomless.

"Yes," she murmured softly, lowering her lashes. Well, it wasn't a lie.

"One day we'll go into that," Brant warned her solemnly.

"But for now—" His knee was wedging against hers and his hand traced possessively over her hip.

"Oh, no!" Vickie protested, laughing. "You have house guests, Mr. Wicker! You planned this thing—by self-admission—and we are going downstairs before Terry has this room dubbed a den of iniquity."

"Damn Terry!" Brant muttered audibly.

"You invited her!" Vickie reminded him wryly, squirming out of the bed and racing for the shower. "Oh, my clothes!"

"I'll get them."

"Put something on first," Vickie called back. "I don't want her jumping you in the hall."

"You are jealous."

"You bet!"

Twenty minutes later they were both respectably dressed in jeans and T-shirts and on their way downstairs to greet the others, Vickie having sworn to keep quiet about the house being Brant's. "I prefer not to give out any of my addresses," he had advised her with a shrug and a grin. "And Monte is hosting this houseful, not me. I intend to be busy."

"Oh?" Vickie queried him.

"With you, spitfire," he told her, swinging her into his arms for a quick kiss. "I did get me a jealous little hellion," he murmured, "but be warned! I can make Othello look like an ineffectual fool if I get irritated myself. . . ."

The feeling of cold dread swept over Vickie again as she scampered down the last steps and cheerily greeted Monte, who was staring out the back sliding doors. Stupid, she told herself. Brant was joking, talking about other men, and there never would be another man. Not for her. Still the weight of her lie hung heavily upon her.

Along with a faint embarrassment that tinged her cheeks pink, she was sure everyone there knew she and Brant had been discovered in bed together. Not that she was ashamed; Brant's love was like a mantle that cloaked her in security. But certain things just didn't need to be advertised.

No one so much as blinked at her. Bobby had taken Terry for

a walk down the beach; the group extolling virtues of the "cottage" consisted of Monte, Connie, and the Blackwells. A few of the others would be arriving later.

"So what's on the agenda, boss?" Vickie teased Monte after kissing his weathered cheek. "Didn't you promise something like a Club Med vacation?"

Monte's gaze flickered briefly from Vickie to Brant, who was leaning nonchalantly over the bannister at the foot of the staircase. Then he looked at Vickie again, realizing wistfully that she had never appeared more radiant. He couldn't even begrudge her a man like Brant.

"Lunch, if you're asking me," Monte said ruefully, his thoughts and feelings hidden as he quickly shuttered his eyes. "That was a long drive." He glanced at Brant again, curious to note that something about his pose was strikingly familiar. No, it was more than his assured stance; it was something about his face. . . .

Foolish, he told himself. Of course Brant was familiar. He was his protégé; now his friend. "Are we eating in or out?" he demanded.

A vote was taken and it was decided lunch would be out; dinner would be a barbecue on the beach. But if Vickie had thought they were just going to join in with the group, Brant was of another inclination. Having staked his claim, he wasn't giving it up for a second. When they forged out to pile into the cars, Vickie was ensnared by his hand, and her place was beside him. She was to his left as they consumed fried clams at a nearby seaside restaurant. And though not obtrusive, Brant's attention was on her exclusively. His fingers would play over the light vein lines of her hands as they sat; his arm was constantly around her waist when they walked.

When they returned to the house, they found that the winds had shifted. With a brisk breeze blowing in from the Gulf, catamaran races seemed to be in order. A variety of small sailboats were rented, and among Brant, Monte, Bobby, and Harry Blackwell—who did know what they were doing—and the others—who didn't know what they were doing—the afternoon became a comedy of errors, one that left all exhausted and giggling over minor catastrophes long after the sailboats had been returned.

Monte, complete with chef's hat, was responsible for grilling the steaks. In his shorts and loud, tourist-type shirt, his skin pink from the day in the sun, he looked more like a happy-go-lucky banker from Pittsburgh on a holiday than a serious director. Maybe a hunter, Vickie thought with a fond chuckle as he wiped his brow and swilled a long draught of cold beer. She chuckled as she approached him with a stack of plates, only to have the sound die in her throat as he looked at her with a curiously stern expression. "I need to talk to you, Vickie."

She raised her hands in the air casually. "Talk!"

"Alone."

Her brows rose in confusion. "Something that serious?"

"I think so." His tone changed instantly and Vickie knew that someone else approached them. "Why don't you take a ride with me in the morning and see what kind of gourmet goodies we can pick up from the fish market we passed today?"

"Sure," Vickie murmured, glancing around to see who was coming toward them.

It was Terry, balancing trays of cole slaw and potato salad. "Well. The vestal virgin in the flesh," she said with a dry smile.

"That's right," Vickie replied nonchalantly, swiping a bite-size piece of potato from the tray. If she let Terry under her skin, she would rub the flesh raw. Ignore her Brant had said. It was on the tip of her tongue to inform Terry blandly that she was going to marry Brant, but she held back. She and Brant seemed to have a silent agreement to say nothing, an agreement that pleased her. The less known, the less that could go wrong.

And Terry, somehow, was a part of that cold dread which would sweep over her. Why, she didn't know. Terry was beautiful and bold and determined. But it wasn't a jealousy over a rival that made Vickie uneasy. She believed Brant saw through Terry's acts. It was something else she couldn't define.

Terry set the tray down and lifted her hair off her neck. "Well," she said sweetly, "if you're not using that room with your luggage tonight, I'll take it. Connie and I were together, but I do prefer to be on my own—"

"She won't be needing the room," Brant supplied, coming upon the group to steal a piece of potato as Vickie had. Still bare-chested in a bathing suit, he radiated a towering strength as he stood among the others. He grinned at Terry, licking mayonnaise off his thumb. "Take the room and make yourself at home!"

For a split-second, Vickie wanted to hit him. Then she smiled. "I hope we don't keep you awake, Terry." Knowing she wouldn't keep a straight face for long, she quickly turned away. Brant followed her; Monte watched the interchange with brooding eyes.

The steak was easily the most delicious Vickie had ever eaten, and yet that was understandable. Her senses all seemed to have reached a new zenith, touched by love and the fulfillment of her dreams.

It was inevitable with their group that someone would have brought a guitar, inevitable that they make a fire on the beach. Inevitable that Brant and Vickie wander off alone.

They strolled along the beach, fingertips touching. Connie, never shy before a small group, was singing a classic love song by Melissa Manchester. The strains of her voice reached them as a private serenade. They stopped and sprawled lazily beneath a low-dipping palm, content to be together in a semi-private paradise.

"I'm proud of you, Vickie," Brant finally said, massaging her nape as she stared out to sea.

"Why?" she murmured.

His grin split wide in the moonlight. "You've learned to ignore attempts to harass!" He chuckled.

She smiled wistfully in return. "I almost told her—"

"Why didn't you?"

Shrugging, Vickie moved into the cradle of his shoulder. "I'd rather surprise her with a deed accomplished."

"Still no faith," Brant answered, stroking her cheek with his forefinger. "Vickie, we'll make it. Couples don't split because of

142

jobs; marriages fall apart because of lack of trust, because people don't talk. That's the only thing I ask, Vickie. Don't ever lie to me."

It was her cue if she had ever heard one, but for the first time in her life, it was as if she had completely forgotten her lines.

Monte was worried; she knew it the moment she stepped into the car with him. He drove in silence for so long that Vickie grew jittery and turned to him in demand. "Would you please say something before I go crazy?"

His glance flicked to her. "Obviously, you and Brant are getting along very well."

"Yes," Vickie said warily, wondering where his line of questioning was going. "Doesn't that please you? It seems to me you've been rather pointedly throwing us together."

"It pleases me," Monte readily admitted, "and I *have* been throwing you together."

"Then what's bothering you?" Vickie asked in bewilderment.

"You."

"Me!" she exclaimed. "Why? How?"

"I know you, Vickie," Monte said solemnly, "probably as well as anyone alive. And I know that something is ripping you up inside. If you don't get it out of your system, you're going to destroy yourself and Brant before you ever get a chance together."

Vickie sat in pained silence, knowing his concern was that of a very dear friend, one determined to help her. And he was right; she needed to talk badly.

"What is it?" Monte persisted. "Are you afraid Brant isn't serious?"

"No," Vickie said faintly. "This is confidential now, but he wants me to marry him."

"And?"

"And what?"

Monte emitted an exasperated sigh. "Are you going to marry him?"

"Yes."

"I know that you're in love with him," Monte said. "And I know he loves you. I believe he has for years. I believe that's the real reason he came back. I didn't call him, you know; he called me."

Vickie glanced at Monte, surprised.

"Yes," Monte repeated, "he called me. It didn't take too long to figure out why. And I'm happy as hell for both of you. You know how much you each mean to me. But Vickie, something is wrong and I know it. I'll figure that out eventually too if you don't tell me. And more important, Brant is eventually going to figure it out too. Don't you think it might help if you talk to me first?"

Vickie should have been on guard, but she wasn't. Monte was her friend, her dear, dear friend, and all he wanted was for things to work out for her. She felt tears spring to her eyes and she opened her mouth before she could think to stop herself.

"Oh, Monte! It's . . . it's Mark."

"Mark! Oh, my God!"

Monte stared at her in silence. Stunned silence. He remembered his earlier thought about the familiarity of Brant. Of course there was a familiarity. It was so plain once he had been told. The eyes. They were the same in the man and the child.

Little streaks of quiet teardrops trickled down Vickie's cheeks. And Monte understood. His tongue felt dry.

"Brant has no idea the child is his?"

Vickie shook her head in wordless misery.

"You have to tell him."

"I can't, not now . . ." Vickie owed him a full explanation, because she cared for him, and because she had now opened her mouth. "Please, Monte, pull over to the side of the road and I'll try to begin at the beginning. . . ."

Monte obediently pulled off the highway, a wise move since his eyes kept focusing on her instead of the road. He listened while she spewed forth a torrent of long-kept secrets, easing her own burden somewhat. He could understand all of her feelings and fears, but as he patted her shoulder comfortingly, he knew it was Brant she needed to talk to, not him.

"You have to tell Brant," Monte echoed as she finished.

"I am going to tell him," Vickie promised.

"Today? When we get back?"

Vickie gasped. "No!"

"Why not?"

"I can't!"

"Vickie!" Monte exclaimed. "You're playing with fire! Granted, Mark looks like you, but Brant is not a stupid man. I would have come around to it eventually, and Brant is ahead of me. He knows . . . uh . . . I mean, he knows there's a possibility. . . ." Monte swallowed and cleared his throat. "He knows he had the opportunity to sire a child."

"I lied about Mark's age," Vickie admitted. "The wedding will be soon," she said in a pleading rush. "I can't tell him until then. Don't you see? It's the same as three years ago. He could marry me now as he would have then just for the child. I have to be sure he loves me, Monte, enough to marry me. If he knew, I would always wonder, and Brant is so—"

"So what?" Monte prompted.

"I don't know exactly what I mean," Vickie sighed, raising her hands helplessly into the air as she searched for the right word. "I just don't know how he is going to react."

"You have to tell him sometime," Monte said philosophically.

"I intend to," Vickie insisted. "I already told you that!"

"When?"

"By the end of the summer," Vickie promised evasively.

Monte looked extremely uncomfortable, and he cleared his throat several times before speaking. "Vickie, Brant is my friend. Please remember that he does have the right to know."

It was the softest of warnings, but she understood its meaning explicitly. If she didn't tell Brant by the end of the summer, Monte would.

"Brant's rights," she said somewhat bitterly. "Monte, what about my rights? Mark is my child—"

"And you just told me that you never gave Brant a chance!"

"Monte, Brant was gone! He was pursuing stardom! What good could have come from my telling him anything? We would

145

have had nothing but an obligation to each other and surely that would have been worse than anything. I never allowed Mark to lack for a thing in the world."

"Except for his father," Monte reminded her.

She was silent as she thought over his words. "All right, Monte, maybe I was wrong. But it doesn't matter anymore. I will tell Brant . . . soon."

He nodded to himself, still looking worried. "Do it soon, Vickie, before someone else—and I don't mean me—does it for you. Someone who figures out you had an affair before . . . and suspects there was no Langley."

"I know," Vickie said softly. "I won't wait long."

"Well"—Monte switched the car's ignition back on—"we'd better go get those lobsters and head back." He grinned ruefully. "I don't want Brant on my tail for keeping you out all day!"

"Monte," Vickie murmured.

"What?"

"Thanks."

"Yeah," he said gruffly.

The guests were playing football on the sandy shore when they returned. Touch football, and Vickie noted dryly as she watched the players from the glass windows that there was a lot of touching going on. Terry had the ball, and she was making certain that she was being touched by Brant. With a pretty laugh and well-executed fall, she tripped in the sand, bringing Brant down with her. The two rolled over together, laughing.

"It was a good fall, don't you think?" Monte queried, and Vickie realized he was behind her, also watching the activity.

"Staged?" Vickie lifted a brow.

"Oh, definitely!" Monte laughed, crinkling his eyes. "I train my people well."

"Yes, you do," Vickie told him, grateful that he had turned the jealousy she had been feeling into amusement. "But tell me, Monte, how many people can see what is staged?"

"The people who count," he said sagely. "Feel like a little touch football?"

Vickie's grin became broad and mischievous. "Sure."

The game endured another hour after Monte and Vickie joined in. Impishly unable to control an urge to torture Brant in kind, Vickie played like a little hellion, having chosen the opposing team. She was careful to be tagged several times by Monte and Bobby, positioning herself so that she eluded Brant's section of the field each time. Until she had a chance to make a touchdown. The goal line being a pair of not quite even palm trees, she was forced to shoot past Brant if she wanted to get the points. She ran like a panther, her feet barely touching the sand, but her effort wasn't quite good enough. Brant didn't merely touch her. She was soundly tackled, imprisoned in his arms, and a recipient of a severe and dark scowl.

"What do you think you've been doing?" he gritted, his face inches from hers.

She could blame her ragged breathing on the run and the fall and she could act as well as Terry. Raising an impertinent brow, she said haughtily, "I was attempting to make a touchdown."

"You know damn well what I'm talking about!" he grated out harshly.

Her eyes widened innocently. "What?"

"You've been in the arms of everyone here!"

"So have you," she reminded him sweetly. "We theater types are a 'touchy' group, aren't we?"

A play of emotions triggered through his eyes, too fast to be read. "Too touchy," he snapped, jumping lithely to his feet and dragging Vickie with him. He kept ahold of her hand while sending the football in a high, spiraling pass to Bobby. "Keep it going!" he yelled. "Vickie and I are going to start dinner!"

"We are not!" she protested, chagrined at his high-handedness.

"Yes, we are," he answered. Giving her no further chance to protest, he lifted her deftly and tossed her over a shoulder. "I'm going to give you a lesson in the fine art of intoxicating lobsters."

"Damn you, Brant!" Vickie screeched, straining from his hold. "I don't intend to be your lackey! Put me down!"

"Momentarily," he replied with determination.

147

He did put her down, flushed and furious, when they reached the kitchen. But when she opened her mouth to lash out at him, he closed it for her quickly with a deep, inescapable kiss. The touch of his full lips elicited the same heady dizziness as always, denying all resistance. Still, her train of thought persisted, and when his lips left hers, she pursed them again to speak. Brant's forefinger fell to them then, silencing her again. The harshness was gone from his eyes and tone as he said, "I don't think either of us is up to football today. We theater types are too touchy!"

"And new lovers too prone to jealousy," Vickie agreed.

"Silly," Brant murmured. "Do you think we'll outgrow it?"

"Never!"

"Control it?"

"Hopefully."

"Definitely, hopefully. I can be a bit of a chauvinistic commando."

"Yes, you can."

"But then, you can be a tease."

"Oh, surely, not purposely!"

He grinned ruefully. "Ha. That was on purpose! Watch the flirting, Ice Maiden, or else!"

"Or else?" Vickie queried.

"Well, actually," Brant countered, taking her hungrily back into his arms, "you shall be a victim of subtle torture. Like the lobsters. Right now I'm going to put them into a huge pot full of beer."

"Beer?"

"Beer. It's only fair that they be sloshed out of their minds before hitting the boiling water."

"Humane torture?"

"Precisely. The meat is also much more tender. The poor inebriated creature hasn't a chance to tense its muscles. It's always best to hit with a ton of bricks when the mind is foggy. Keep that in mind."

Brant didn't notice that Vickie's smile had all but disappeared. He had released her to pop the cans and pour beer into a huge cauldron in preparation for the feisty crustaceans. She was taking his words to heart. One day soon she would be doing her best to get Brant very, very "sloshed." And hopefully his muscles wouldn't tense.

He was, however, as tense as a piano wire when he returned her to her house the next day, holding her as tightly as a long-lost treasure. "Less than a week," he murmured, "and I'll never let you go again."

"You don't have to let me go now," Vickie whispered into his chest.

Her words had a straightening effect upon him and he set her away from himself firmly with a rueful shake of his head. "Mark is due home soon, and he may be only two, but I'm marrying his mother before I move in with her. And you have a show tonight, and a rehearsal tomorrow, and we have to get a license tomorrow and *Othello* will open with us as newlyweds—need I go on!"

"No!" Vickie chuckled, careful not to touch him again lest she cling and demand he stay with her. She frowned suddenly. "Brant, can we keep the marriage secret for a while?"

"I guess it would be a good idea," he agreed, smiling as he touched a finger to her forehead to ease the lines. "We should have a little time before being hit by the publicity. Monte is going to have to know. I'd like him to be a witness. And I'd like to be married at Frankie's by the beach, if you don't mind. We can have a small reception with plenty of Dom Pérignon."

"Perfect," Vickie told him with wide eyes, catching his finger wickedly and nibbling on its tip while watching him. "Monte already knows. I told him."

"Stop that," Brant threatened, pinching her cheek as he snatched back his finger. "Or else your son and brother will return to a very indecent scene!" Grinning, he headed for the door, only to halt and add, "Well, I'm glad you told Monte but what about your family? Would you like your brother and his wife at the ceremony?"

"No!" she said quickly, too quickly. "I mean, I'd like this very small. Just us. Please?"

"Fine, I just thought . . ."

149

"Oh, I am close to Edward. Very close. I really can't explain it, I just want the ceremony to be small."

Brant shrugged tolerantly. "Then small it shall be." He was gone then, and Vickie shortly had reason to be grateful. Edward appeared with Mark.

After she had greeted both him and her son, and after Mark had scampered off into his own room, Edward was on her with the demanding familiarity of an older brother. Only her father could have quizzed her with more presumption. "I want," he said flatly, "to know what that was all about."

"What?" she made a play for innocence.

"Don't give me that, Victoria," Edward insisted, fuming. She wondered for an idle moment if perhaps she hadn't been mistaken. Edward was much better at paternal indignation than even her father was. "I know, sibling dearest, that you are a superb actress. But the act doesn't work on me because I know that you're acting. Why did you throw me out of your house when I picked up Mark?"

"I didn't throw you out of my house!"

"Yes, you did. You would have done so literally if you could have!"

Vickie glanced at her fingernails and then studied them as if she expected to find an answer in their shiny color. Her teeth began to work on her lips, and then she tried to stop the involuntary action. Edward would also recognize it as a sign of her guilt. She couldn't stop the gnawing though, and she came to another quick decision. Edward was going to get that answer soon, and if he happened to be around Brant, his surprise would give it all away. But if he knew, if he understood, he would willingly make sure not to be near Brant until she had her chance . . . her right moment.

She was in for a lecture. One much worse than Monte's. But she had to get it over with eventually, and each time she admitted the truth, perhaps she would gain strength for the ultimate revelation. . . .

"Mark is Brant's son," she said bluntly, tonelessly, not looking

150

at her brother. "I was afraid you'd figure it out and give me away."

She heard his long, indrawn breath. His reaction was similar to Monte's. "Of course. It was right there in front of me." Suddenly he spun on her. It was lecture time.

"And you still haven't told him!"

"No, I—"

"Oh, Vickie! I always supported you; I always stood by you. I thought you had sensible reasons for what you did."

"I did, and do—have sensible reasons!" Vickie blurted out.

She wasn't sure Edward even heard her outburst. He continued. "Brant Wicker is a responsible man, Vickie; he would have married you. He would have taken care of Mark. Been there. I never pressured you, Vickie, because I thought you had some sound decisions made. I thought the real father might have . . . might have . . . oh, I don't know! Been killed. Been a petty, sad infatuation, one you had quickly gotten over, a dropout . . . some kind of a real bum, skid-row type—"

"Thanks, Edward," Vickie interrupted dryly. "I'm glad you have such faith in my taste."

He stopped for a moment to stare at her in confusion, and then flushed slightly. "All right, not skid-row, but you know what I mean. Some kind of a young guy with no sense of responsibility, someone who really wouldn't care. But Brant Wicker isn't that type—"

"I didn't realize you knew him that well," Vickie interrupted again.

Her words didn't deter him this time. "I know *of* him," Edward said with a gray glower. "And he can't be too terrible if you're seeing him again."

"Edward, he isn't terrible at all! I'm very much in love with the man, and always was." With a surge of agitation Vickie left the sofa, where she had been calmly sitting, and restlessly plucked a cigarette from a box she kept on the coffee table, tapping it lightly before she lit it. Inhaling deeply, she stifled a cough and turned back to her brother. "Edward, Brant will know now, in time. I'm going to marry him."

151

"Before you tell him about Mark?"

"Yes."

"Victoria—"

"Don't Victoria me, Ed! Think about it. Would you like to wonder if you'd been married because of a child?" Vickie demanded point-blank.

"Oh, Vickie—"

"Would you?"

"Of course not, but he's already asked you," Edward reminded her.

"I know." Vickie was pacing the room like her brother. She made herself stop, realizing that the scene between the two of them could have been taken straight from an old Tallulah Bankhead movie. "Edward," she told him honestly, "I'm scared. No, Brant isn't a bum. He isn't terrible. He's wonderful to millions of people. Think of who he is, Ed. This marriage has to be so very positive! Less than fifty percent of normal marriages work out. In Hollywood—"

"This isn't Hollywood, and I doubt if Brant Wicker lives the usual Hollywood life-style."

"Oh, Edward," Vickie moaned, "please try to understand."

"Vickie." Capturing her shoulders, he smiled into her eyes. "I do understand. I just want you to think very hard about what you're doing."

Vickie slowly returned his smile. "I have thought, believe me. I've gone into self-inflicted mental torture over the whole thing!"

"Okay then, lecture is over. When is the big day?"

"Soon. We're having sort of an elopement and keeping it secret awhile," Vickie told him, brightening.

"Damn!" Edward suddenly marveled. "I just realized that Brant Wicker is going to be my brother-in-law! Damn!" he muttered again, shaking his head.

Vickie chuckled. "Stardust, brother?" Not thinking, she repeated Brant's words. "He is a man, Edward. Not a star in the heavens—a man."

But during the week Vickie began to think of Brant as an unreachable star again. Rehearsals became grueling as opening

152

night for *Othello* approached and, other than the few hours they stole away together to acquire their marriage license, she didn't see Brant alone for a second. Costumes were worn to rehearsal; props came into use. Even the set was taking shape behind that of the *Godspell* flats. And on Friday, they went to full makeup. Even Vickie was shocked when she first saw Brant with his hair rinsed black and his skin stained to a deep bronze.

The effect was astounding. He was Othello the Moor. Strong, resolute uncompromising, his performance as vivid and energetic as the blue of his eyes against the stain of his skin.

There was dead silence when the curtain fell, then Monte's excited reaction as it reopened with the cast anxiously waiting onstage. "Damn, that was good! We're ready for an opening!"

Cheers rose on the stage, and everyone began congratulating everyone else, especially Brant. He didn't shy from compliments, but rather turned them around. "Othello is nothing without a striking Iago!" he said, shaking Bobby's hand. The two men unabashedly embraced as Roman legionnaires might, old friends come together again in a moment of glory. But Brant's salutes did not end there. He went on to include the entire cast, exalting even the college students hired as the extras. "This has been said a million times, but no part is so small that its execution can afford to be less than a real part of the whole. Our production is a tight one because every spoke in our wheel is turning."

Monte's grin could be seen flashing white from the darkened table where he sat. "I think Brant said just about everything. But don't pound your backs too hard yet. Tomorrow we'll have two full dress/tech rehearsals. They will be slow ones—I want to adjust a lot of lighting. Tomorrow night *Godspell* closes. Tuesday afternoon is our last rehearsal, a run-through with no flaws, please. Tuesday will be opening night for the press." His tone had grown severe, but he ended with another ear-splitting grin. "Right now I think we'll break out some champagne. . . ."

Brant and Vickie were still by the bed where she, as Desdemona, had just been smothered by Brant, as Othello, because of her supposed infidelity, egged on by Iago. Brant reached for her hand as the others filed offstage to change. His grip was a firm one, pulling her into an embrace. "I forgot to mention what passion for an indisputably sexy and gorgeous Desdemona could do for the performance of an Othello!" he whispered wickedly.

Chuckling, Vickie chastised Brant. "Let me go, mighty warrior! Everyone will be watching."

"They won't see a thing they don't already know."

Vickie squirmed from his arms hastily. She still carried an admonishing smile upon her lips, but she really didn't care what others saw. She was dressed in a filmy white gown—Desdemona's nightgown—and Brant's touch through the light-as-gossamer fabric was more than she could stand at the moment. The heat and strength of his entire body seemed to sear through her, and it had been a long week, with Brant staying chastely away, especially after the reawakening of her yearning.

"Behave, Othello!" she commanded him impertinently.

"What?" he demanded in sardonic reply. "Are Desdemona's eyes straying already?" He pointed to the bed; the scene of the tearjerking confrontation of the play. "See what happens to errant wives?"

"Ah, but she wasn't errant. Othello made the mistake of listening to others."

Laughing, they moved offstage together. Watching from the darkened house, Monte sighed. They were an extraordinary couple, above mere humanity as they stood together beneath the lights of the stage—he magnificent in the royal cloth of gold, she a creature of ageless beauty in the flowing white gown, her raven hair waving down her back in thick, lustrous swirls. They were magic. So intense, so vital. Their being was a tangible thing that radiated around them. They lived passionately; they loved passionately. They would quarrel passionately.

Monte sighed again as they moved into the wings. He hoped Vickie knew what she was doing.

There was a portent of disaster in the air. Portent. Monte shook his head. He had been doing Shakespeare too long. He was beginning to think with a medieval mind! It was foolish to think that anything could go wrong.

CHAPTER EIGHT

They were married on Sunday morning, with a high, brilliant sun above them and the gentle rolling of the surf behind them. Vickie was in yellow, challenging the radiance of the sun; Brant wore a deep blue that turned his smoldering eyes to a depthless indigo. Only Monte and Frankie and Mrs. Leonini—and the minister— stood witness, they and the swaying palms and bleached sands that Brant and Vickie both loved so dearly.

Edward was the only other person with an idea that a marriage was taking place and he was once more caring for his nephew in St. Petersburg. If he resented his role in the proceedings, he gave no sign. Vickie was the actress, not he. He knew he would not be able to conceal the secret he had stumbled upon.

Vickie had no thoughts for her own secrets that morning. She was entranced with the dazzling beauty of the day, and with the simple promises of the ceremony. To love, honor, and cherish. They were words she could easily avow to. She had loved him in her heart forever. The depth of her love was also to take on new meaning when Brant's eyes met hers with the words "Till death do us part." There was a message in his tender look, a message as old as the sky and sea that blessed their union. He believed in forever. For better or worse.

And when he kissed his new bride, it was with an aching tenderness, broken only as Frankie chuckled and cleared his throat. "When do I get to kiss the bride?" he complained.

"Now," Brant declared dryly. "And then forever after, you can hold your peace!"

Even Monte seemed lighthearted as he kissed Vickie and

wished them both the best. "I look at it this way," he said with a grin. "I'm not losing an actress; I'm gaining an actor."

"That's right," Vickie promised solemnly, throwing her arms around his neck to hold him closely. "You'll have us both whenever you want."

"Good," Monte said gruffly, "because we may be taping *Othello* for the PBS stations. I'll need you both."

"So where's the honeymoon?" Frankie demanded as he popped the cork off the neck of a champagne bottle and passed out crystal glasses.

"That is a deep, dark secret," Brant advised, his eyes dancing devilishly. "But take my word for it—no one will be able to find us until Tuesday!"

Actually, they planned to honeymoon at Vickie's house. Like laughing kids they parked both cars at a nearby garage, turned the phone down too low to be heard, and settled in for their short time of complete privacy. They didn't have forty-eight hours before Vickie was due to pick up Mark. Then she and Brant would both be due for opening night.

Vickie was unaccountably assailed by a case of nerves as they entered the house. "Seems warm, doesn't it?" she murmured, whisking quickly to the thermostat.

Brant was right behind her, his arms encircling her waist. "It is warm, Mrs. Wicker," he said huskily, "but I don't think you're going to cool anything down that way!"

Vickie slowly turned in his arms. "Oh, Brant! I'm so happy, I can't believe it's real!"

"I'm real," he retorted, "and I plan to start proving it. We have a lot of honeymooning to get in to a very few hours. . . ."

His fingers tingled her spine as they danced from her shoulders to her waist, and she swayed dizzily against him. "Too much champagne," she murmured apologetically.

"Thanks," he chuckled. "Married an hour and you already consider my lovemaking skills to be an overindulgence in spirits!"

"Never!" she told him, meeting his eyes as his fingers worked on her zipper. The yellow dress fell to the floor and she was swept with pleasure at his response.

Brant had little control over his senses where she was concerned. Seeing her each time anew was a marvel for him; his pulse immediately quickened, his breathing grew rapid. But she was beguiling, an enticement of the blood. Clad only in delicately laced lingerie that seemed nothing more than a tempting froth of white, she was definitely a temptress. The French-cut bra enhanced rather than hid the high firmness of her breasts, scarcely veiling the roseate peaks that darkened swiftly, as if blushing at his surveillance. The silky slip gave further credence to the perfection of her hips, the willowy length of tanned, sleek legs.

He kissed the erratically beating pulse at the base of her neck, then swept her into his arms, laying her tenderly upon the bed in her room, the yellow gown forgotten in the hall. She watched him through half-closed, sultry cat eyes as he doffed his own jacket and twisted his tie from his neck, but then she lay still no more. With graceful fluidity of movement, she came to her knees on the bed, clasped his face between her hands, and kissed him, drawing away only as the embrace threatened to consume them. Her eyes fixed upon his shirt, as feather-light fingers deftly slipped buttons one by one through their buttonholes and she leisurely pulled the tails from his trousers, running her hands with fascination over the incredible flatness of his belly.

"God!" Brant groaned as her lips found his chest and her tongue lashed a delicious torment over his flesh. "Woman, you're driving me crazy!"

He expelled a shattering breath and she was catapulted into his arms as his weight swept her back to the bed and his lips claimed hers. Then he trailed a path of desire grown fervent over her throat, the soft flesh of her arms, the mounds that rose majestically over the top of her bra. It was then time for all constraining fabric to go; without awkwardness Brant paused only long enough to remove sensuously her sheer slip and panties, and his own trousers and briefs. Neither was concerned with the haphazard strewing of their clothing.

157

"I love you," Brant whispered hoarsely, lowering his weight as he kissed her lower lip, nibbling it erotically. "I love your face"—his kisses rained upon it—"I love your neck, your breasts, your legs. . . ." His kisses followed his designations, gaining blazing heat with every assertion. Vickie tried to retaliate, but she was quivering like a blade of grass in his raging wind of desire, and as his kisses moved upward over the agonizingly sensitized soft flesh of her upper thighs, she cried out, begging him to take her. He was thirsting, ready to comply; her return of torment was an innate thing, making him wild. It was in her hips that naturally undulated for him, the legs that slid along his length, willing prisoners for his maleness, the breasts that pressed to his chest, arched, the nipples exotic bewitchment as they teased against the coarse hairs, giving . . . receiving. . . .

"Brant . . ." Vickie moaned, her whisper a further taunt to whirling abandon as it whistled against his ear with moist fire. She was not hesitant to guide him, not averse to groaning her pleasure as he took her hips firmly to guide in return.

It was impossible, but being together in the total oneness of the senses was more exhilarating, more awesome, more all-consuming than ever before. Did a piece of paper promising commitment make it so? Vickie wondered briefly. No, not the paper. The hearts that joined together to make the commitment made it so. It didn't matter. The primitive beauty that drove them wildly, insatiably, together needed no definition. Morning turned to afternoon, afternoon to evening, and after the first whirling vortex of tumultuous appeasement, the passage of time became meaningless. They were alone, an island, giving heed to nothing but the precious moments of each other, playing all the games of love, whispering, demanding, surrendering. He would seduce her; she would seduce him. At times they would madly join together, at times they would sweetly torment each other until one would capitulate and demand in return.

It might be swift, it might be simple, but Vickie knew she would cherish the memories of her "honeymoon" all of her life.

Finally they lay contentedly together, Vickie resting her head on Brant's stomach, drawing idle circles with her thumb over his chest. Brant was strangely silent, and after a while she stretched to kiss him quizzically.

"Penny for your thoughts," she murmured, then added playfully, "You look engrossed. I'll even offer a quarter."

The intensity of his brooding eyes quelled her initial curiosity. Too late she realized that his questions were going to come.

He stroked her hair, watching the tendrils as he would release them. "I want to know about the past, Vickie. Surely you trust me now. I want to know about everything in your life since I went away."

Her lashes fluttered over her eyes and she moved her head back to his stomach, staring at the ceiling. "Brant," she finally said, "please, not today."

"Vickie." His voice held a note of sternness. There had been something in the wedding ceremony about "obey," and Vickie winced slightly. It seemed Brant was also taking that word to heart.

She closed her eyes tightly and repeated, "Oh, Brant, please! Not today. Today is ours; it's special. Let's keep it that way." She hadn't really intended to, but instinct had sent a quivering note of beseechment into her voice. It was a feminine ploy she wasn't fond of using.

Brant's touch on her hair hardened almost imperceptively, and then relaxed. "Do you trust me, Vickie?"

"You know I do," she murmured, concealing the misery his question brought. She did trust him. Almost. But not enough to take the kind of chance he was asking of her on this particular day.

"And you do intend to really talk to me soon?" The slight tightening of his hand again warned her that any promise she made to him would be one she would be forced to keep.

"Yes," she said, biting her lower lip. "Soon, Brant, I promise. But please . . . not today."

His stroke became a light one. "All right, my love, not today. But you will talk to me soon. You're still hiding something, and that bothers me. I don't like you living with this fear—it makes me uneasy."

Vickie twisted and talked into the rigid wall of his stomach. "Oh, Brant! I do love you, and I do trust you. Please, don't worry. . . ." She worried enough for both of them. She was afraid, and terribly uneasy herself. But there were magical moments when she could convince herself that everything was going to be all right. Today had been a euphoric combination of many such moments. "I'm not really hiding anything," she fibbed. "There's no reason to be uneasy." If only she could believe that herself!

Brant sighed, and she felt his movement constrict his muscles even more tightly. "Vickie, you could ask me for the moon today, and I'd try to find a way to give it to you." He sat up suddenly, and cradled her head in his lap. He grinned as he stared down into her eyes, and she knew that the subject had been closed—temporarily. "Since you're not asking for the moon, and I don't have to go running around in the buff trying to get it, how do you feel about a little physical fulfillment?"

Vickie's eyes widened in reproachful amazement. "If you're not fulfilled . . ."

"Oh, I am, I am!" he countered, ruffling her hair as he chuckled. "But I'm also ravenous. I'm so fulfilled that I've worked up a tremendous appetite—for food."

"Nice," Vickie teased, "married less than a day, and when you say you're hungry, you're already talking about food."

"This time!" he warned, arching a brow questioningly. "But if you feel I'm disappointing you, I can promise that if you flick that wicked hair of yours over the section of my anatomy upon which it's resting one more time, I'll be more than ready to keep practicing another kind of appeasement!"

Laughing at the seductive threat in his eyes, Vickie bolted up, deeply content with the naturalness of their nakedness, but quick to heed his warning and slip into a concealing, downy-soft, floor-length robe. She was equally quick to toss Brant his slightly rumpled pants, aware as she watched him that his threat had not been an idle one.

"Come on, starving one!" she commanded, wrinkling her nose

at him as she pelted for the bedroom door. "We'll raid the refrigerator together."

"What?" he grumbled with mock amazement. "I've got myself a wife and she doesn't want to cook for her new husband?"

"Damn right!" Vickie called. "This is a partnership, even if you are rich and famous. This is my honeymoon too."

"That's all right," Brant called, padding behind her to sweep her into his arms and spin her in a circle. He held her high in the air and gave her a self-satisfied smirk. "I'm probably a better cook anyway!"

"Ha!" Vickie grinned mischievously, loving the face she looked down into. "But I promise to give you plenty of chances to prove it."

"The matter is actually irrelevant," Brant said, setting her down and arrogantly slapping her rear. "It's obvious we're going to need a full-time housekeeper."

It seemed incredible to Vickie when she woke on Tuesday morning that she was going to leave Brant if only for a few hours. As he had once walked into the theater and begun to dominate her life, he had now walked into her life and was dominating her being in the most wonderful of ways. He was a demanding man, but he asked no more than he gave. As his wife she would always toe a tight line, but he made no secret of the fact that he was equally tied to the line. Theirs would never fall into the category of an open marriage.

Rising carefully so as not to awaken Brant, she almost tripped over one of his valises. He still hadn't finished unpacking, having decided he could do so when Vickie went for Mark. They had spent their time so engrossed in each other. She had been amazed when they talked to discover just how wealthy he had become, then humbled with a touch of special pride for him; he had several houses in the United States, and a few abroad, and yet he was content to call her small place home.

She watched him as she dressed; she would never tire of watching him. Even in his sleep he exuded a magnetism. Then, before picking up her purse and leaving, she gave into temptation and kissed his lips. He shifted, settling deeper into the covers, but did not awaken.

She tiptoed slowly, backing away from his sleeping form, suddenly poignantly remembering the last time, almost three years ago, when she had left him like that. It had been so pathetically different! She had left him with the sure, agonizing knowledge that she would never see him so again, her heart in shatters, her mind building a defensive wall.

Today her heart was singing with happiness. She had all she could ever want. She would return and see him again, lay down beside him at night, rest her head on his strong shoulder when she grew weary.

She left him with a tender smile of serenity.

He was gone when she returned. A note tossed on the neatly made bed simply read *Gone to the theater.* Vickie wasn't alarmed at first, merely disappointed and puzzled. Why had he gone in so early? Monte, Vickie thought, narrowing her eyes with anger for her director. Monte probably had some problem and called Brant in to help. Damn him! He knew they had so little time.
. . .

She spent the afternoon playing with Mark. As dinnertime rolled around she set the table for three, hoping Brant would walk back in, but he made no appearance. She thought about calling the theater, but then decided she had waited too late. She would be there herself shortly.

Rushing into the busy theater's dining room forty-five minutes later, she looked feverishly about for Brant but saw no sign of him. She considered a trip to the men's dressing room to pull him out, but Jim cornered her and nervously sent her dressing herself. A few minor adjustments still had to be made on a costume. She became immediately immersed in the excitement and bustle of opening night.

She didn't see Brant until they were onstage together, and consequently, she didn't know anything was wrong until they walked into the wings. His touch upon her was like cold lead, and he released her the moment they reached the sheltered shad-

162

ows of curtains and flies. Bewildered, slowly filling with dread, Vickie tried to study his face, but it wasn't a face she knew.

It was severe, rock-hard in the shadows, the prominence of his cheekbones, square line of jaw, and arrogant length of nose all made more chillingly visible by the mahogany stain of the make-up and the ink black of his hair. In the austerity of his dark, savage scowl, his lips were little more than a thin, ruthless line. His eyes raked over her like daggers of crystal. His voice was a whiplash as he dropped her arm, stared at her with those daggers, and ignored her tentative "Brant—"

"Madam, I will talk to you at home." With a slight inclination of his head he crossed his arms and strode away from her to hover near Jim's podium.

Alone in the curtained shadowland, Vickie fought the panic that engulfed her. She wanted to run after him and shake him and demand to know what was wrong. But she couldn't. A few feet away the play was going on. She had to pull herself together. She had a quick costume change and then the next scene.

The play had never gone better. The tensions that coiled on the inside of Brant and Vickie found the right channels in their Othello and Desdemona. Their timing was perfect, the pace fluid. And as the show neared its end, the murder scene was nothing short of brilliant. Laying silently as Brant rendered his soliloquy to her sleeping form, Vickie knew in a portion of her mind that the audience of critics was spellbound.

Anyone who had ever loved, known heartache and betrayal, could empathize with the character. She could almost feel the audience, completely caught in the magic, held back merely by the barrier of footlights from telling Othello that he was making a grave mistake.

His lips, as he kissed her in sleep, a gentle farewell before the deed, were cold as lead. His monologue continued. "One more, and that's the last. . . ." His lips touched hers again, infinitely soft, but so deathly cold. This the last . . . It took all her years of training to remember it was a play. She wanted to open her eyes, to demand to know what was wrong. The line rang so very truthfully. Was it her last kiss?

"This sorrow's heavenly, it strikes where it doth love. She wakes."

She could finally open her eyes, the actress in control, playing a scene passionately and brilliantly, mesmerizing the audience with ardor and vibrancy.

But for Vickie it was a nightmare she lived, swearing a bewilderment and innocence that was ruthlessly ignored. Othello would kill his Desdemona rather than be betrayed. Love twisted to horror.

"Kill me tomorrow; let me live tonight!"

Her line was a passionate plea from the heart; his rejoinder equally adamant. As staged, she was swept into forceful arms and sent back to the bed with a poignant combination of lost tenderness and agonized resolution. His hands hovered over her threateningly, and for the briefest of seconds, she lost herself in the illusion. His eyes were so pained, so brilliantly condemning.
. . .

But of course, it was all make-believe. He was perfectly controlled. The audience's eyes cruelly affixed on her—her throat, her flesh, not feeling the slightest pain.

Moments later she came temporarily back to life to speak her final lines, then fell into the death pose she would hold for the completion of the play. The stage came alive with activity; Iago was proved the villain and wounded, Othello went into his suicide monologue and fell heavily across her to die. Lodovico delivered the closing lines.

The applause was deafening; the players were rewarded with a standing ovation.

Brant smiled as he jumped to his feet to lead Vickie and Bobby forward for the curtain call. But his eyes, when they rested upon her, were still blue ice. The smile was as much an act as the murderous passion.

It was bedlam after the show. Reporters had come from all over the globe because of Brant, and it was hours later that the interviews and pictures ended. Monte was in his own seventh heaven. Catching Vickie for a moment in the confusion, he tapped her chin affectionately with elation. "Every director's dream!" he exalted. "They're saying this might be the finest production of the play since the Bard produced it himself!"

Vickie smiled weakly. She was thrilled for Monte, for the play, for her fellow actors. But she felt that she had never left the shadows. Nothing had fervor or taste without Brant beside her, and the only time he came near her was to uphold the priorities of picture taking. And now he had disappeared. When she had changed back into her street clothes, she loitered around the men's dressing room, only to learn from Bobby that he had already gone home.

"I wouldn't see him tonight if I were you anyway!" Bobby said cheerfully. "He's in a hell of a mood."

Vickie blanched slightly. Bobby didn't know that she had to see Brant. The home he had gone to was her own.

"Did he say anything?" she asked quietly.

Bobby shrugged. "You know Brant. He never says anything. Just clams up and gets away as fast as he can."

"Oh," Vickie murmured, lowering her eyes as she realized that he was watching her suspiciously.

"You look pale," Bobby said, concerned. "Want me to take you for a drink?"

"No, no, thanks, Bobby," she said quickly, her voice faint. "I guess I'd better get home myself."

He was waiting for her, still as death as he sat in the darkness, his very stillness made ominous by the fury that exuded from him like a tangible, crackling tension. Vickie closed the door behind her and leaned against it, watching him warily as she grasped for support, her knees grown weak.

He stayed silent for so long, a part of the darkness with his hair still black and his skin still stained, that Vickie feared the tumultuous pounding of her heart would cease altogether and she would sink to the floor. Then his voice thundered a single word with the ferocity of a bullwhip.

"Well?"

Her mouth was cotton, too dry to allow her to do more than stupidly rasp "Well, what?" in return.

He rose with the violent wrath of a volcano erupting, heedlessly knocking his chair to the floor as he did so. He stalked her with vehement strides and none too gently grasped her arms to toss her to the couch, ignoring her faint cry of alarmed protest.

"Don't worry, Mrs. Wicker, I have no intention of causing injury to that alabaster skin," he ranted, glaring down at her with his fists jammed into his pockets. "I just thought you might like to sit, since I think you have a few rather lengthy explanations to give me."

Her mind was working a mile a minute, but she couldn't form a single word. What had happened? How could he know anything?

"What's the matter, Mrs. Wicker, no script planned for the occasion? No lines to rattle off? Think of the sofa as the stage. Here's the scene: irate—no, no, that's too tame—furious husband has discovered a serious oversight of sweet, secretive new wife. It seems she has forgotten to tell him about something, *someone*, who surely must be deemed important. So there you are, Victoria Langley, stage and scene. Adlib the lines. Perhaps you'd like a drink first? I'd rather like one myself." A few swift strides brought him to the swinging kitchen doors, where he paused for a second to turn back to her mockingly. "Amazing how a dead man like myself could need a drink. I mean according to you, as Mark's father, I am dead."

He returned a minute later to thrust a snifter into her hand. Brandy. She did need it; her entire body had gone numb. Brant righted the chair he had knocked over and sat again, studying her, his legs crossed negligently, one hand twirling the amber liquid in his glass, the other held prayer-fashion against his lips. Vickie's fingers trembled as she sipped the brandy, then swallowed it down in one burning gulp, her head vociferously pounding out the word *how*.

"Talk, Vickie," he commanded in a dry grate.

His malevolent, dangerous glare was driving her crazy, but denial now would be a level less than foolish. Somehow he did have his facts straight. "What do you want me to say?" she finally croaked in a faint whisper.

"Good Lord, woman!" he bellowed scornfully, his fingers leaving his face to dig into the arm of the chair as he struggled for control. "I want you to explain *why*. Why didn't you let me know three years ago? Why did you marry me with that kind of a lie? When were you planning on telling me? At my son's college graduation? Or perhaps you didn't trust me? You were never going to tell him, assuming in that sweet little mind of yours that something could go wrong and I might still insist upon sharing my son?"

Each question lashed into Vickie with a painful bite. Her heart felt as if it sank from her body and lay bleeding at her feet. He hated her now. She had been wrong . . . or had she? His reaction was the one she had feared. She had laid herself bare for this agony. Stiffening her spine, she rebuilt her crumbling defenses. "I didn't have your phone number in Hollywood," she told him sarcastically, "so it was rather difficult to tell you anything."

"Don't give me that!" Brant growled, "I had a right—"

"You had a right!" Vickie said in a shrill voice springing from the couch to glower over him, shaking with the intensity of her fear and anger. "No! I had the rights! You were gone—you were busy becoming a damned star!"

He stood and she instinctively stepped back a half a step, a grim twist coming to his lips. "You knew me better than that, Vickie. I would have come back, I would have taken care of you."

"You idiot!" she charged, digging her nails into her palms and fiercely biting her own lip to keep back tears. "I didn't want to be taken care of! I could take care of myself."

"And Mark?"

"Yes!" Vickie cried, "and Mark!"

"You're a righteous little bitch, Vickie," he said coldly.

"How dare you!"

It was all she could say. He breached the few feet between them in a whirl and gripped her shoulders tightly to flounce her back to the sofa and hold her there this time, his hands irons that imprisoned her, his eyes blazing into hers. "Bad question, Mrs.

Wicker," he admonished her icily. "And don't move that pretty little rump of yours again. I'm not through."

"I am!" she challenged, unable to stop her body from shaking like a leaf in a high wind. "You can just leave me alone. I knew you'd behave like this!"

"You knew it? When did you know it? When I came back? When I told you I was in love with you? When we made love? When you married me? When did you know it, Vickie, when?"

She dropped her head, but he lifted her chin back up. "Damnation! It was bad enough that you hid this from me at the beginning. Brave little girl!" he scoffed. "Having her baby alone! Sorry, it smacks of a little cowardice to me. Moralistic snobbery. You couldn't give anyone else credit for caring, concern, or a sense of values. Dependability. Responsibility. Or love."

He released her shoulders in disgust with a slight shove, and paced to the middle of the room. His back was to her when he spoke again.

"But I can understand that, Victoria. I would give my right arm to go back and undo it, but I can understand it. I was gone. You were frightened. What I can't understand is how you could have married me, sworn to love, honor, and trust me, with that kind of a lie in your heart."

"I was going to tell you!" Vickie cried out.

His powerful shoulders shrugged in answer. "Like I said, Vickie, when? On my son's twenty-first birthday? Or perhaps when he was inducted into the army?"

"I was going to tell you this week," she said miserably, wanting to run to him or into the night but knowing both would be futile. "I—I couldn't tell you before the wedding. I couldn't take a chance."

"A chance?" he railed incredulously. "A chance on what?"

"On your marrying me because of Mark . . ."

"Oh, Lord, what an excuse! I had already asked you!"

"Yes . . . but . . . but . . . oh, never mind!" Didn't he know how terrified she had been? How uncertain? How pathetically in love? Obviously not. She raised her chin. "How did you find out?"

"A little matter of a birth certificate."

Vickie gasped, and stood again in anger. "You bastard! You went snooping through my house—"

"I think I suggested you sit!" Brant interrupted savagely, capturing her in a fierce embrace that brought them both breathlessly to the couch. Brant extended his length over hers and pinioned her arms above her head as she uselessly struggled against him. His expression was harsh and fathomless; he didn't attempt to talk again until she went limp against him. "I wasn't snooping, Mrs. Wicker, merely unpacking. I didn't realize you hadn't intended the top bureau drawer for me. And I must have been blind as a bat before, but since you had lied about his age, I simply didn't see. Just out of idle curiosity though, how many people know that I have a son?"

"Two," Vickie muttered through clenched teeth.

"Who?"

"My brother and Monte."

"And how do they know?" Brant enunciated crisply.

Vickie stared at him blankly for several seconds, weighing her answer. She had told Monte because he had been concerned and she had suddenly found herself desperately needing to talk . . . to release tension. She had told Edward rather than allow him to guess the truth at an inopportune time. But either way, *she* had *told* them both, and she hadn't been able to tell Brant. The answers sounded pathetically weak in her own mind.

"I believe I stated the question clearly," Brant grated.

God, she wondered, still not speaking, still not blinking. He was angry now, and might become so much angrier. Perhaps she should lie again . . . tell him that they had guessed.

"Vickie! I'm waiting for an answer!"

His vise around her wrists tightened convulsively and Vickie gasped, blurting out the truth. "I told them!" The lies had gotten her into this position to begin with. Another, she realized vaguely when the words were out, would weave another web and build more tension, and, besides, what difference could it make now?

"You told Monte, and you told your brother." Brant stated her admission incredulously. "And you didn't tell me."

169

"Yes." She said it simply, too despondent to attempt an explanation. She had had her reasons, terrible fears, but now with the relentless intensity of his furious face above hers he was never going to understand, never going to try to understand.

"You didn't tell me," he repeated almost tonelessly. "Why bother? I'm only the father," he murmured sarcastically. "Have all these confessions to the wrong people been recent?"

She sighed and chewed at her bottom lip. "Yes, since you've been back."

"God, I really was a fool," Brant berated himself with a brittle laugh that brushed her ear with warm breath. "The last to know, they say. . . ." His eyes bored into hers, blue fire. "That child is going to carry my name, Vickie, and not by adoption. We'll take every conceivable blood test and hire every lawyer in the country if that's what it takes. You've kept him from me for over two years, but I'll be damned if I'll ever let you do so again."

"No!" she screamed in panic. Her worst nightmares were coming true. He was going to leave her, and he was going to try to take Mark. "No!" she screamed again, her voice rising shrilly in the silent night.

Brant tensed as if he had been shot. "Shut up!" he commanded Vickie harshly. God, how could she still deny him? He had given her his love, his trust, his soul, his life. She was his wife. His anger was pain, and each word she coolly spoke twisted a knife farther into him.

And still he wanted her. She was irrevocably his, even as she railed against him. He could feel the soft firmness of her form beneath him, her harried breathing brought her breasts crushing to his chest, her stiff defiance melded her hips to his. Her eyes flashed like gray storms while her lips parted to deny him once again.

He smiled suddenly, a grim smile that didn't reach the ice of his eyes. Then his lips swooped down to muffle the sounds from her. His kiss was a bittersweet combination of tenderness and savagery, love and agonized anger. She attempted to twist her head, but he held her still, commanding response as he plundered the depths of her mouth and availed his hands of the curves beneath him. A familiar heat began to pound through him.

Abruptly, he wrenched himself from her, striding swiftly for the door in his haste to hide the unsteadiness of his stance and gait. He had to get away from her. God, he was about to rape his own wife! A wife who had lied to him, betrayed him, denied him. Who now cried innocence while still denying him. Wasn't she? She was dead silent now; she hadn't moved. But she still intended to keep him from his own son. . . .

A shudder rippled through him and he bit down hard with his teeth and rolled his hands into tight fists. He stood like a ramrod. "Sorry about that," he said with cool indifference. "I thought I should remind you that you are still my wife."

In a haze of pain and longing, Vickie knew only that he was standing by the door. He was leaving.

She closed her eyes, willing no tears to flow. "Fine," she said flatly. "I'm still your wife. Go on. Go wherever you were going."

She heard the door slam.

CHAPTER NINE

Vickie awoke slowly the next morning, stiff and cramped. For a moment she wondered why; her dreams had been sweet, she had nestled with her new husband through the night. No, she hadn't. Brant had walked out, and sometime after he had left, she had risen to drag herself into Mark's room. She was cramped because she had fallen asleep with half of her body draped over her son's bed. He still slept, a lock of raven hair swept over his brow.

Vickie stood and tried to stretch the kinks from her body, hoping against hope that she would move out into the living room or kitchen and find Brant busily doing something. Hoping that he had returned later . . .

But of course he wasn't there. He would have never returned and left her half on the floor. She had to face facts—he wasn't returning.

She was grateful for the responsibility of motherhood that morning; it kept her from falling apart. It made it imperative that she function, shower, dress, care for her son, all without resorting to hysteria or a deluge of tears.

And because of Mark, she made it to the theater dry-eyed, refusing to allow herself the luxury of worrying about the future, or what would happen next. Brant didn't make idle threats. He would drag her into every court of the land.

The excitement in the theater upon her arrival temporarily swept the tumult of her personal disasters from her mind. The reviews were in, and the least exalting of them called the production "a brilliant masterpiece." Monte, high on a cloud of glory,

172

was giving the cast members time to read the papers while they consumed coffee and doughnuts. Vickie picked up the nearest one and began to read. The bulk of the praise went to Monte and Brant, but she and Bobby had also been singled out for exceptional praise. The *Sun-Times* reporter proclaimed her "an actress of infinite depth, talent, and beauty," who "created a character of ethereal charisma who stole the heart." Nice, Vickie thought, silently thanking the writer for his words. Her ego could use the boost.

Her skin prickled and she felt herself flush. Brant was behind her. His spicy masculine scent was warning of his presence long before his hand touched her shoulder.

She whirled away furiously, remembering the words that had passed between them, the miserable night she had spent, and how he had forcefully inflamed her body, bruising her lips, reducing her to quivers and longing, only to walk out into the night. And not return.

"Don't jump from me like a damned rabbit!" he hissed, mindful of being overheard. "I want to talk to you."

Vickie assessed his features quickly for any sign of forgiveness, hoping against hope. But she could see nothing in his implacable eyes or grim tight lips. The blue that measured her in return was opaque, challenging, frightening.

"You did enough talking last night," she snapped scathingly, sickeningly aware that she was widening the breach between them to dangerous bounds. She didn't seem to be able to help herself, but she didn't want to hear his words. If he still loved her, he would have come home last night.

What he wanted to talk about was Mark, and sharing him in the future. And she didn't want to hear it . . . not now . . . not while her heart was still being torn piece by piece into little shreds.

"You are going to listen to me, Miss Langley," he insisted, reaching for her arm with another of his binding grips. "I realize that discussion and honesty are not your cup of tea, but there is the future to be settled—"

"Hey!" Bobby cheerfully interrupted, such a whirlwind of

exhilaration he didn't feel the tension between the couple he accosted. "Have you read the Jacksonville paper yet? This guy sounds like he's ready to call New York and insist we get every Tony Award out!" He paused suddenly, studying Vickie's white face. "Lord, Vick, you really had better read it. You look like you could use some good news."

Vickie didn't get a chance to reply, nor did Brant. Terry sidled up to them next, casually casting an arm around Brant's shoulder as she picked up on Bobby's remark with a saccharine smile. "Poor Vickie! Didn't you sleep well? You really do look ghastly!"

Vickie did her very best to return the sickly sweet smile. "I feel absolutely ghastly," she muttered, quickly jerking her wrist from Brant's grasp. "I'm afraid I might be coming down with something. I'm going home. Tell Monte to call me when he can with any of his last-minute changes or instructions, will you?" Not waiting for assent from anyone, she turned and fled, aware that Brant would probably come after her, but determined to elude him or die in the process. Without looking back, she whipped open the Volvo door and slammed it hastily behind her as soon as she was seated, immediately hitting the locks.

Brant did follow her. He shouted and banged on the glass with a force she feared would shatter the window, but she ignored him and put the car into gear, revving the engine. Practically stripping the gears, she jerked the shift into first.

It might be foolish to run from things that had to be faced, but at the moment, she simply couldn't face Brant Wicker. She needed a little more time to lick reopened wounds before raising the shield of indifference she would need for the confrontation that would come. Time to build an implacable strength.

Brant followed her to the house, but by that time she had barricaded herself in. He had his own set of keys, of course, but she had bolts and chains in place. She could hear him cursing; she could hear the shrill of the doorbell as he leaned against it relentlessly. But the nightmare in her mind was louder. He didn't want her anymore, but as she had always feared, he did want their son. He had walked out on her, but now he wanted to discuss Mark calmly. She was no longer safe behind the wall of his ignorance. Nor could she keep Mark from him any longer. It would be wrong for the child, and she knew it. She accepted it. She just couldn't deal with it until she had somehow glued together the tattered remnants of her heart.

The shrilling of the bell finally ceased. Vickie took two aspirin and bathed her face in cold water. She laid down until she could stop herself from shivering, her fingers from trembling. Then she called Monte—practice again!—and apologized coolly for missing the critique session that he considered so important before the real opening night whether they had received high praise from the press or not.

Vickie had never missed a day before. Not a show, not a rehearsal, not a critique. She explained that she had felt desperately ill, but was fine now. It was the truth, she told herself, or would be by the time she had to report back for the show. Monte sounded concerned, but not suspicious. Apparently Brant had said nothing to him.

Vickie spent the rest of the morning rehearsing her own private final scene, the meeting with Brant that she could not run from after the show. She would have to be dignified and not burst into tears, she would have to convince him she would play no more games but allow him to see his son—on her terms for the good of the child. He was too young to be uprooted, even for a month or so in the summer. Brant would have to come to Sarasota specified times, times when Vickie could disappear and Edward could be there with his nephew to greet Brant.

She left the house tentatively when it was time to pick up Mark, afraid that Brant was waiting for her. But he was nowhere in sight. Nor was he at the school. Nor did he attempt to call her, or come to the house again.

He had probably decided the hell with his futile efforts. He knew he would be able to corner her at the theater. The complete break could come tonight, and again she would feel as if part of her body had been severed. But at least now she was better prepared. Her star had been within reach, but she had gambled and lost. It had moved farther and farther from her grasp, and the insurmountable problem she had tried to ignore had exploded in her face. So much for dreams. They died along the wasteland of reality.

Eventually it was time to return to the theater. Vickie drove in with her eyes bone dry and her back as straight as one of Smoky's plywood flats. She even called cheery greetings to the others as she made her way to the dressing room, careful to keep her vision from falling directly on Brant, not wanting him to accost her before the show. But Brant ignored her. From trying to pound down her door like a madman, he had made a complete turnabout. His role was now one of an indifference as staunch as her own. She caught his eye just once, fleetingly. And he smiled, a grim smile, a smile full of purpose.

She turned away quickly. That smile told her everything in a nutshell. There was going to be no more running away. He was going to get her—tonight.

Everything about the theater was so normal, Vickie thought as she set about applying her makeup as she had hundreds of times. There was the usual chattering in the dressing room. Terry was in an especially good humor, and tried to draw Vickie out. There wasn't anything malicious in her bantering, and Vickie realized she had been foolish ever to worry about Terry. The brunette was simply a sultry beauty who liked men. She would have never infringed upon the depth of love that had been Vickie's with Brant. But it didn't make matters better to know she had dug all of her own holes.

Life went on, Vickie told herself stoically. And if she could endure this night, she could surely endure anything.

In the wing as the show opened, Vickie closed her eyes and forced herself to concentrate on her character. She rolled the name Desdemona over and over on her tongue, recalling early acting lessons. Be a tree. Be a bird. Think tree. Move bird. Be Desdemona, walk Desdemona. Think and talk Desdemona. And she did. The wheels began to turn. The play was on. Brant was Othello; she was Desdemona. Moving fluidly from scene to scene, act to act. To the end, murder most foul. Brant's corpse falling over hers.

Applause. The beautiful, thunderous sound that actors lived

for. Then would come the curtain call, and the peace of solitude. Maybe she could evade Brant for one more night. He had left her last night. Perhaps with the excitement he would leave her again.

Brant's left hand was gripping hers as they moved to the footlights to bow to another standing ovation. The curtain fell once, and Vickie tried to retrieve her hand. The curtain went up one more time. Vickie wound her facial muscles back into a rather sick smile for the still standing audience. Her mind wasn't with them. When she had tried to extricate her fingers from Brant's death grip, she hadn't been able to budge them. Thoughts of running again were swept away. Tonight, in a matter of minutes, they would have to decide what to do, how to dissolve all ties between them, how to handle Mark.

The curtain fell for the final time. Vickie jerked madly at her fingers again, and glared at Brant with a trembling hostility when he refused to let go. He ignored her, and turned to the others still milling onstage, as if they had been previously asked to stay.

They had been asked to stay! Vickie realized quickly as Brant began to talk. Vickie felt herself go clammy with fear. He was going to make an announcement about Mark, she thought with sick terror. Right here, right in front of everyone. Oh, God, no, please, she prayed silently, don't bare my heartache to an audience. She couldn't believe Brant would do such a thing, but she knew he was headed for something.

"This is a very special show for me," he was saying, his beautiful grin starkly displaying perfect white teeth against the mahogany of his makeup. "For several reasons. One, I began my career here, with the help of a brilliant man, Monte Clayton."

The cast began their own round of affectionate applause for Monte, who Vickie saw blushing slightly in the wings. It didn't surprise Vickie that Brant should direct the praise for his success to Monte; relating in such a way was part of the charisma that was Brant Wicker. But still she knew something else was coming, and she braced herself for it, mentally and physically. No matter what he said, she would hold her head high. She would get through it. It was coming. . . .

"Something else began for me here," he continued pleasantly, and Vickie was aware she could barely hear the sound of breathing, perhaps her own respiratory system had simply stopped. Brant turned to her, his blue eyes vivid against the darkness of his face. "Something even more important than my career." He was an actor, he couldn't resist a dramatic pause, but that pause almost killed Vickie. Get it over with! she silently screamed. He began again.

"Three years ago, without even realizing it at first, I lost my heart to this lovely leading lady. I admit, I came back here for more than a show. I came back for Vickie, and this time around, I won her for good. She consented to be my wife. I'd like to take this opportunity to share our happiness with you and announce that our marriage took place three days ago."

She couldn't have remained standing if he hadn't been there to support her. What was he doing? she wondered desperately as a gasp escaped her, luckily covered by the eruption of applause, whistling, and hearty congratulations from the cast. Was he playing a new game, or was this real? How could he walk out on her, ignore her, and then calmly announce that they were married? A combination of soaring joy and the fear that it would be immediately snatched away caused her to turn on him waspishly. "What do you think you're doing?" she hissed, her voice audible only to him as she wrenched herself away, backing warily from him. He advanced on her as she moved, slowly and surely, keeping pace as she kept backing away. He was laughing, and she quickly realized why. Her sightless meanderings were a sad mistake. She backed herself all the way to Desdemona's stage bed and found her knees buckling, her form sprawling gracelessly upon it. Heedless of those around them, Brant leaped beside her and pinioned her there. "I was going public," he declared. "It seemed the only thing to do when you wouldn't listen to me."

The others were quickly around them and Vickie didn't have a chance to say any more as she rose to sit at the edge of the bed. The entire cast had enthusiastic congratulations to give, kisses for Vickie, handshakes for Brant. Bobby, being closest to them both, was the most vociferous. Terry, too, seemed wildly excited, which momentarily surprised Vickie. Until she discovered why. Brant had made good his idle musings and introduced her to Frankie, who was waiting to take her to a late dinner.

"I'm just crazy about Italians!" Terry whispered to Vickie while Brant was distracted by another well-wisher. "They do make the sexiest lovers!" she cooed. "Maybe we can double sometime!"

"Sure," Vickie smiled, "I'd like that." She wondered briefly who would rule that roost and laughed inwardly with imaginings of the battle for supremacy between the two.

The stage remained alive for several minutes longer as people chuckled and chatted, the drama of real life at its best. Then one by one the players began to filter to the dressing rooms, until only Vickie and Brant remained, eyeing each other silently on Desdemona's bed.

"I want to make an apology," Brant said gruffly, then demanded, "and then I want one in return!"

Vickie's tongue felt like lead. "You really want to stay married?" she asked thickly.

"What?" he growled. "Of course I want to stay married, you little bonehead! I told you once that marriage was forever to me! If you had any thoughts of dissolving any commitments to me, you had better forget them fast! You're my wife, from now to eternity."

She wanted to touch him so badly, to be held by him, to grieve together for past mistakes. But a remnant of fear stayed through the joy and relief slowly filtering to her conscious mind. "Brant, you left me!" she accused him.

"I was angry, very angry," he admitted, his eyes bare to hers. "But I shouldn't have walked out. I'm sorry, very sorry. Now do I get my apologies in return?"

He was half teasing, and she knew it, but his love came through in his constricting touch, his voice, the eyes that bored into hers. She wanted it all out. She wanted to hold him in return.

"Oh, Brant," she murmured miserably. "I really don't know where to begin. It's just that I always thought I was right. In the beginning I had no idea that you cared for me. I was in love with you, and I would have stayed with you that night three years ago except that you said, 'I love you,' but not to me! You said it to Lenore. So when I found out about Mark . . ." Her words trailed away.

"Lord!" Brant groaned, wincing. He ran a finger tenderly over the outline of her lips. "What a thing to have done to you! I didn't realize . . . forgive me! Love was just a word to me until that night. I tried to see you again, but you wouldn't give me the time of day. Then your memory kept haunting me, so I came back. I knew you were on your own with a child. Monte told me, and I prayed you might want me now that you were a few years older. You were so cool. I never guessed about Mark. And then when the evidence slapped me in the face, I was crushed. I'm thrilled that he is my son. But, Vickie, I was hurt. I couldn't believe you didn't trust me enough to tell me. Actually"—he smiled ruefully—"I left because I wanted you so badly it was killing me and I needed badly to simmer down."

"I wanted you too," Vickie admitted, trembling fingers dipping into the dyed black hair on the head that hovered over hers. "I thought that you hated me," she whispered, "that you would never forgive me."

"Foolish," Brant whispered back. "An argument doesn't stop love."

"But you walked out—"

"I tried to come back, but you must have bolted the door before falling asleep. I was afraid too, Vickie. I just couldn't make you trust me! I thought you wanted out, and that you wanted to deny me Mark. I thought about a few of the things I had said, and knew I had to talk calmly. I took time to think. That's something you're a little poor at too, my love."

"Thinking?" Vickie flushed and clasped his hand to bring it to her breast. "I acted abominably today, I guess, refusing to trust you enough to talk."

"You certainly did!" Brant agreed, chuckling. "How dare you, after all those lies!" With mock severity he warned her, "Oh, what a tangled web we weave, when first we practice to deceive!"

"Shakespeare?" Vickie intoned with a quirk of her brow, a

slow smile slipping into her lips. "Haven't we had our quota for the night?"

"Not Shakespeare!" Brant groaned. "Your knowledge of quotes is also poor, Victoria, but I suppose I can overlook that fault. Sir Walter Scott."

Vickie giggled. Brant was staring at her with an innocently academic look while finding fascination with unobtrusively kneading fingers in the plunging valley between her breasts where she had drawn his hand in comfort. "Oh," she murmured, lazily enjoying the sensation of his touch before frowning. "Brant, I am so sorry. So sorry about everything."

"Vickie," he returned intently. "I'm sorry too. I hit you with the blow you were expecting, going into a fury like that. But it's all out and over now. We both understand the tightropes we were teetering on. We have everything going right for us now, loving each other, believing in that love. And we have a beautiful son, two good careers. I think we're remarkably lucky people. I want all sorrys to be in the past. Except"—his eyes danced mischievously—"feel free to apologize for any dumb moves you make in the future. We are going to argue now and then, but I won't walk out again, and you won't start planning the divorce!"

"Agreed!" Vickie chuckled, then her temper flared. "Dumb moves that I might make! What about you—"

"I knew we'd argue, with your temper!" Brant sighed.

"My temper!" Vickie saw the twitch in his lips and dissolved into laughter.

"Oh! I forgot!" Brant kissed her quickly. "Say you're sorry for one last time!" His free hand swung as if to tap the exposed side of her rear end, but the sharp, teasing slap became a caress. Vickie jumped in surprise and yelped a protest that became an endearment. "Don't cajole me, Mrs. Wicker!" Brant feigned chastisement. "I insist you promise to never, never mistrust my capacity for understanding again!"

"I'm sorry!" Vickie added hastily. "One last time!" Her voice became a serious vow. "And never! I will never again mistrust or doubt anything about you! I love you." She clutched the fingers that taunted her flesh through the sheer gown. There were still things that had to be said. "Brant," she asked slowly, "what about Mark?"

He sighed and looked her steadily in the eye. "He is my son, Vickie, and I love him, as I do his mother. I loved him before I realized who he is, and I think you know that. In this state we can go back and legally change his name. When he grows up, he'll never have to doubt either parent." He touched a finger to her chin to deeply study her eyes. "The papers may get wind of it, Vickie. Will you be able to handle the publicity?"

A soft, sultry smile was forming on Vickie's lips. "I don't care what is written or said, as long as I know that you love me, and Mark, and that we're all going to be together. Mark is the important one, and he does deserve his father. And speaking of Mark, don't you think we'd best head home to our son—and our own bed? Desdemona's is a little lumpy!"

Brant looked like the reincarnation of the devil then, ice blue fire dancing in his eyes against the sinister darkness of his Othello makeup. He sprang from the stage bed, pulling her with him. "Home sounds wonderful. I'll need a long, long bath"—he nibbled the corner of her ear erotically—"but that sounds enticing too. My darling wife can help me wash this makeup from all over my body!"

"It's all over your body?" Vickie inquired teasingly.

"Well," he admitted, his words muffled as his nibbles moved down the length of her throat, "not *all* over my body but we'll pretend that it is!" He left off his nibbling and abruptly gave her a playful smack on the rump. "Let's have no more of this, woman! Let's change and go home!"

They met outside the dressing rooms and arm in arm left the theater slowly. It was empty now; the others had gone while they dawdled on the stage. There was a cast party to celebrate the opening of *Othello* somewhere, but once again, neither of them would be going.

Brant halted with his hand upon the switch for the entry lights. Pulling Vickie into the circle of his arms, he brushed a kiss on the top of her head, inhaling the sweet scent of her hair.

"Why are we stopping?" Vickie asked a trifle breathlessly. She could see nothing of interest in the rows of empty tables.

He grinned and pulled her closer. "I was thinking Shakespeare again."

"Oh?" It was a mere whisper; she was thinking nothing but Brant, and anticipating a long hot bath together and exploring fingers on each other's flesh.

"Ummm," he replied, spinning her to fit harmoniously against his form and assail her with a rough kiss that left nothing of his own desire hidden as their hips pressed magnetically together. "I have a suggestion for Monte's next show," he whispered when he released her. He switched off the lights and led her into the night that welcomed them for their homeward journey.

"All's Well That Ends Well."

Vickie laughed delightedly. "Most fitting, Mr. Wicker."

"Yes, Mrs. Wicker, if I do say so myself."

EPILOGUE

She wasn't young as she stood at the door that night, not young in the sense of complete innocence. She was at a beautiful age for a woman, approaching thirty, tall, lithe and shapely, confident in herself, happy with her world. She knew where she was going, she knew what she wanted, and above all, she had the confident assurance of loving, and knowing she was loved with equal fervor in return. She was a career woman, a mother, and most important, a wife.

She was dressed in a stunning, sultry, silk sheath. Her hair was midway down her back, a fan of softness to put the feel of the silk to shame, styled in layers that flattered large gray eyes and a slender, arresting face that was both demure and worldly. She was cool, capable of handling herself, a picture of the ultimate dream of sophistication. But her gray eyes and full lips were friendly, smiling; she was known as being pleasant and gracious, totally unaffected. The things said and written about her pleased her, and yet they left her with wonder. It was so easy to be pleasant! She knew what many had learned and many still sought —that loving and sharing was the magic potion to making everything else wonderful, palatable, and even tragedy, bearable.

She had come with the full intent to seduce. He was her dream, her life, her existence. And tonight she would be with him. It was, however, a special night.

He opened the bedroom door, a puzzled expression mingling with that wonderful male appreciation he never failed to give her. If they lived to be eighty, and if she were wrinkled like a prune from head to toe, her beauty faded to all other eyes, he would still give her that look. She smiled. When his golden hair had turned pure white and age had crinkled his face to a thousand lines, he would still be magnificent to her.

He kissed her forehead and allowed his eyes to roam from the top of her well-groomed head to the tip of her elegantly shod toe. "You look gorgeous beyond description." He flattered her lavishly, his eyes warmly amused and devilish. "But why are you knocking at your own door?"

Vickie chuckled and spinned into the bedroom, returning the assessment, feeling a quiver of anticipation assail her. Brant was one man who could really wear a tuxedo. He was masculine and rugged, yet elegant and beautiful in the sheer physical sense of the word. "I dressed in Mark's room," she said with a slow smile, spinning again, this time a graceful movement that brought her into his arms. "Does the dress remind you of anything?"

"My love," Brant teased, welcoming her into his embrace, "I have never been accused of a faulty memory." Her head was tilted up at him and he smiled into her eyes tenderly. "I remember very clearly the night a little raven-haired waif appeared at my door in blue silk to pull me up when I was down. It's a very special, precious memory. But why tonight?"

Vickie sighed with mock exasperation. "Brant! It's clear to see you've become an old married man—no romance! And your memory is faulty! This is our anniversary!"

Brant frowned. "We were married in July and I remember it's our anniversary each year without fail!"

"Not that anniversary!" Vickie whispered, still marveling at the feel and scent of him as she burrowed into his broad chest, the rough material of his jacket a caress to her cheek. "It was exactly seven years ago tonight that that little waif appeared at your door!"

"So it was," Brant chuckled, threading his fingers through the black hair that fluffed like angel's wings on his lapel. "But my darling wife, my romantic one, why are we celebrating tonight when we have neglected to do so in the past?"

"Wellll . . ." Vickie drew away from him to meet his eyes. "For one, we're back in Sarasota." It was a special night because they were being honored at Monte's by the governor of the state for a theater arts festival. "And two, the stage is set. Monte will be there, and Bobby and Terry. There's going to be a cast party, which we will have to attend, but only briefly! And three . . ." A slight blush rose to Vickie's cheeks, making Brant marvel at his wife in return. She had handled success and the viper pit that was part of Hollywood and fame without ever changing her sweet inner self or losing that trace of innocence that proclaimed her completely his.

"Go on," he encouraged softly. "What's three?"

"I read an article in one of those fan magazines today," she grinned. "It said we were expecting a child, and at first I laughed, but the more I thought about the idea, the more I liked it! Mark is six now, if he's ever going to have a brother or sister . . ."

Brant laughed delightedly and pulled her back into his arms. "I think we should oblige whatever magazine that was. But are you sure? Your career is skyrocketing."

"Yes," Vickie said demurely, "I'm sure no one will forget me after only nine months. Besides, with your help, I'll never need to worry about work!"

"Good point!" Brant agreed, and Vickie gasped as she felt his hands on her back and heard the whistle of her zipper as it was released. In a deft, split-second movement, Brant slid the sheath from her shoulders and it fell to the floor in a soft puff at her feet.

"Brant!" Vickie squirmed as her flesh crushed deliciously to him. "I didn't mean right this second—"

"You sound like an old married lady!" Brant whispered, his voice a warm rush of air that caressed the lobe of her ear. "No romance." His fingers played a seductive tune down the hollow of her spine that both tantalized her and divested her of her slip. "Our son is with his uncle—"

"The awards banquet!" Vickie interrupted weakly.

"—is still an hour away," he finished for her.

Vickie's arms curled around his neck and her fingers twined into the golden fringe of hair at his nape. "So it is!" she said complacently, drawing his head to hers to lock his lips against her own with sweet invitation. Their embrace lasted a long time,

lovers still in love, attuned to the needs of each other, wonderful-
ly, openly, aware as a heat formed in each to combine and soar
into a consuming flame.

"Our clothes!" Vickie mumbled feebly when they broke and
her fevered fingers helped with the removal of his tuxedo, quivering as they came upon his bare flesh.

Brant chuckled, a throaty, deep sound in his chest. "We have
an iron here somewhere . . . I believe . . ." He stepped over her
silk sheath and abruptly swept her into his arms. "This is far
more romantic for an old married couple, don't you think?"

"Umm . . ." Vickie was swimming in sensation, on a celestial
cloud of wonder. It was amazing, after all these years, but the
touch of her husband could still send her soaring to the heavens.

"Brant," she murmured as he brought her to the bed and sent
her writhing with longing when his tongue taunted her peaking
nipples. "I had this all planned . . . uh . . . out for later. I was
. . . oooh, Brant . . . going to order Chinese food . . . and, uh,
uh, the whole bit."

His answer was muffled against the hollow of her hip. "We'll
do the whole bit later! We're older now, you know. We may need
a lot of practice to come up with a sister for Mark."

"Oh," Vickie agreed, her hands convulsively gripping Brant's
shoulders.

He moved over her and took her lips again, then smiled into
her eyes, his devilish, riddled with desire, and also a stern warning.

"One thing, Mrs. Wicker."

"Yes?" Vickie inquired, only halfway paying attention as she
was feeling the crushing, demanding heat of his body against
hers.

"You leave the bedsheets alone tonight and—" His arms tightened around her "—you don't dare leave this room! You may be
a star to the world, Mrs. Wicker, but Mr. Wicker will happily
tan your famous hide!"

"Bad publicity," Vickie teased.

"Victoria!"

Arching her body more closely than ever to his warmth, Vick-

187

ie smiled. Her voice was a whisper of silk against his flesh. "I've no intention of leaving, Mr. Wicker, not ever again."

"I love you, Vickie."

What marvelous little words, haunting, tearing, exhilarating, adoring. All their meaning in a name. The right name, the right man, the right woman.

"I love you, Brant."

Candlelight
Ecstasy Romances™

Candlelight
Ecstasy Romances™

$1.95 each

"No. Just...no." Taking another step back, almost tripping over her feet, Emily willed Cortez to leave, but he didn't move. And try as she might, she couldn't break away from his dark, steady gaze. It shackled her to him as securely as a set of chains, holding her prisoner in a place as unfamiliar as it was alluring.

It was the crash of Danny's bicycle as he dropped it to the driveway that finally freed her. He called to her from across the lawn.

"Hey, Mom, I'm home."

Her son was bounding up the porch steps before Emily, senses reeling, could say another word. She watched Danny's bright blue eyes, Eric's eyes, as he studied Cortez and the dog. He sidled up alongside his mother, his tumble of honey-blond curls brushing against her arm. Then, with a huge grin that took both adults by surprise, he held out his hand.

"Hi. I'm Danny. Who are you?"

With complete and utter fascination, Emily observed the changes that took place in Joseph Cortez as he greeted her son. He focused his attention on Danny, his features softening. A smile warmed his fierce, dark eyes and turned up the corners of his mouth. Bending slightly to accommodate himself to her son's shorter stature, he extended his hand.

"Hi, Danny. I'm Joseph Cortez."

Instinctively Emily wrapped an arm around her son's shoulders, but instinct also warned it was already too late. Danny's small hand rested in Joseph's larger one, the clasped hands drawing them to each other, leaving Emily feeling very much the outsider.

Danny had never been a shy child, but he was cautious, rarely warming up to strangers on the first meeting. With Cortez he was displaying more interest and enthusiasm in a matter of minutes than he'd yet to show Glen Roberts, the

man she occasionally dated. In fact, from the way Danny
and Cortez were looking at each other, one would think each
had found a long-lost friend.

"I'm six, and I'm going to first grade next week," Danny
offered, in answer to some unspoken question, as he withdrew his hand from Joseph's. "Why are you here?"

"He was just leav—" Emily began in a determined tone
of voice, but Cortez neatly cut her off.

"I'm going to be working with Professor Mendoza at the
university, and I need a place to live. I saw the sign on your
front lawn, and thought I might be able to stay here."

"Oh, yeah? Neat. Do you draw pictures like the professor?"

"Yes, and I paint, too."

"Will you draw a picture of me?"

"Danny!" Emily protested, her hand squeezing his
shoulder in warning.

Man and boy leveled such fierce frowns at her that Emily
caught herself shrugging apologetically. Let them talk all
they want, she thought, as she dropped her arm to her side.
Cortez was *not* moving into her house, no matter how in-
triguing he was, no matter how much she needed the money,
no matter how nice he was to Danny.

"Of coursé I'll draw a picture of you," Joseph promised, as he turned his attention back to the boy. Try as he
might, he couldn't quite keep the triumph out of his voice.
He'd found the key to her, and he'd be damned if he wasn't
going to turn it. For her, not against her, he thought, feeling the need to justify his position—for her and Danny, and
perhaps most of all for himself.

"Is this your dog? Can I pet him?"

"Yes, she's my dog. Her name is Greta, but before you
pet her, let me introduce you, all right?"